Sugarcoated

Deception

Book 1 of the Deception Series

by London St. Charles

LS Charles Publishing Group

Chicago, Illinois

LS Charles Publishing Group
www.londonstcharles.com

Sugarcoated Deception by London St. Charles Copyright ©2019
Trade Paperback ISBN: 978-0-9993288-8-0
E-Book ASIN: B07MT85Y54

Cover Designed by:
Gisele Marie: www.authorgiselemarie.com
Interior Designed by:
Gisele Marie: www.authorgiselemarie.com
Editorial Consultant:
Naleighna Kai:www.naleighnakai.com

Acknowledgements:

Praises to the Almighty for giving me the gift to create and the ability to use it, through Him all things are possible.

Sugarcoated Deception came about by accident. I was working on something else and couldn't get my thoughts together. I had a deadline with no vision or direction in sight (a bad position to be in). Then a tragic and heartbreaking incident happened to someone I know. I crafted a fictional story loosely based on that event, drawing from the raw emotions I felt as the circumstances unfolded. I wrote with so much feeling that I found myself in tears at times. The words flowed from my fingertips to the keyboard, resulting in a dynamic story. Ironically, this was the easiest writing I have ever done (by accident).

Many thanks to:

The man whose last name I share, thanks for always cheering me on. Mom, thanks for doing what you do best … loving me and my dreams. For reading my excerpts and offering your honest opinions. I'm overjoyed I get to share my writing journey with you. Shanda & Sharon, for listening to me go on and on about my writing and never sounding annoyed or uninterested.

Gwen, for our plotting sessions. Girllllll, we got mad chemistry. Your input in this story was major.

My literary family:
One word sums you all up ... TRIBE!!! I am blessed to be part of this circle of sisters and one brother of the pen. We rock!!!

The readers:
Thanks for purchasing my books, spreading the word, and posting reviews. Know that your support is appreciated.

One Love,

London St. Charles

Dedication:

To Priscilla Jackson, my very first beta reader.
Your sweet spirit and kind words are missed.
RIP
She LOVED this story.

About the Author

National bestselling author, London St. Charles has always had a passion for the pen, paper, and books. She is a Chicago native who uses the Windy City as a backdrop to the romance, suspense, and contemporary fiction stories she writes. London published her debut novel, The Husband We Share in 2017 and is one of nine authors in the anthology, Sugar. London also has a novella, Betrayal of Trust, releasing early 2019. She composes an online newsletter, London Writes, that keeps readers abreast of what's going on in her world.

FOLLOW LONDON ON SOCIAL MEDIA
Facebook: London St. Charles
Instagram: london_writes
Twitter: @LSCharles2017

Chapter 1

Four words would put an end to Cadence Goldsmith's perfect life.

"That's Mr. Goldsmith, Mommy."

She searched out the source of that small childlike screech, an unnatural occurrence in the Adali Global Reveal. The event was an exclusive affair for people who worked in the European auto market.

Cadence peered around the velvet curtain from her spot backstage of the McCormick Place Convention Center, surprised to find that her husband, Jackson, and mother were sitting in the front row next to a scowling Steven Bekker, her work nemesis. But that child's voice, which cut through the hum of conversation at an event, honoring Cadence's major achievements, was out of place.

"Hiiiiiii, Mr. Goldsmith," a little girl with light-brown skin, translucent blue-eyes and puffy blonde twists crooned, as she rushed to stand near her husband. "You work at my school."

Cadence grimaced, stumbling backward as the curtains swayed toward opposite ends of the stage. Why was a child there and why was she so interested in Jackson? Wait, was that an image of her husband on that child's shirt?

"I present to you, CDO, Cadence Goldsmith."

Cadence straightened the blazer of the red power suit she'd paired with a cream camisole, and pointy nude heels that adorned her petite frame. Her curly hair was straight and slicked back into a ponytail. She adjusted her classic pearl necklace, swept away the building anxiety within, and smiled.

Applause rang out as she strutted center stage with her attention on the bleached-blonde woman wearing a navy dress, who grinned and winked at her before taking an empty seat next to Jackson and pulling the little girl onto her lap. Jackson glanced at Cadence, then frowned as he put his focus back on the woman. She didn't miss the panic that took over his features for a split second.

Cadence's heart surged with a bit of panic of her own. Nothing good was going to come of these strange set of occurrences. She prayed that her confidence would still show through, even though relishing the acknowledgment of being the designer of the first self-driving automobile was taking a back seat to Jackson shifting in the chair, her mother peering at him and then the child as though putting two and two together and coming up with fifteen.

Michael Zornig, Adali's CEO, handed Cadence the microphone and she whispered, "Thanks for bringing my family. It's a nice touch."

"You're welcome," he responded moving his short-round frame to the opposite side of the stage as the overhead screen descended from the ceiling.

Annoyance had set up residence in her body. Jackson, who seemed occupied with the distraction that little girl had become, hadn't acknowledged Cadence at all. The wonderful gesture on Mike's part was all for nothing. She forced a pleasant expression as she observed Jackson and the woman have a heated but whispered conversation. Jackson's body language—tense and angry—screamed discomfort.

The little girl sat quietly and picked at the glittery letters on the front of her yellow t-shirt with an iron-on picture that Cadence still couldn't make out clearly because part of it was scrunched in the girl's fist.

"May I have everyone's attention please," Cadence said walking to the edge of the stage, standing in front of

Jackson.

The scent of Tom Ford cologne made her body tingle. A thousand men could wear that same fragrance, and she could pick out her husband blindfolded every time.

Jackson's brown eyes gazed into hers, but the comfort and security she usually felt were missing.

"Mommy, now," the little girl asked in her outside voice.

"Shhhh." The woman placed an index finger to her thin pink lips. "Not yet."

Cadence raised an eyebrow, then glanced at her husband, who shrugged.

The lights dimmed, and Cadence began the PowerPoint presentation of the newest addition to the Adali luxury car fleet.

Cadence Goldsmith was the youngest Chief Design Officer and automotive engineer to date. She was the only woman to hold that position in the history of the company. The fact that she was a Black woman under thirty and one of the highest paid executives, made everyone take notice. Most times, she'd been mistaken for a car saleswoman until someone addressed her as Ms. Goldsmith, then heads turned, and jaws plummeted to the floor.

Ten minutes later, every person, except for Steven and the mystery woman, were on their feet clapping. Cadence had dreamed of this moment. She had made her mark in the global market. Her life would never be the same and neither would her salary.

As the room illuminated, Mike lifted a hand to settle the crowd. "Cadence Goldsmith has a bright future with Adali, and we, along with the two most important people in her life, her husband, Jackson Goldsmith, and mother, Phylicia Kerrington, would like to present her with the Outstanding Innovative Design Award."

"Yay, Mr. Goldsmith," the little girl squealed, slapping her hands together. Cadence's attention was drawn to the child whose eyes matched the woman she assumed to be her mother. High heels clicking across the stage accompanied by Jackson's signature fragrance snapped Cadence from the trance.

"We appreciate your hard work," Mike said handing a black and gold plaque with the Adali emblem engraved in the center of it to Cadence.

"Thank you." She shook his hand trying to play it cool even though she wanted to shatter the surrounding windows with a high-pitched scream.

"Congratulations." Jackson beamed with cautionary excitement written all over his face as he embraced his wife.

"Who the hell is that woman," she whispered through a clenched-teeth grin as her lips brushed the side of his ear.

Jackson's dark-skin ashen. "Her name's Braelyn," he replied, planting a soft kiss on her cheek. "We'll talk later," he said, pulling away with a matching plastic smile.

Her mother stepped forward and tilted her head heavenward, lifting her chin. "Your father would be so proud of you." She took a breath, pushed her shoulders back and chest out. Cadence followed suit, although her heart was pounding out of her chest. The women stood there strong and confident in solidarity.

"We here at Adali appreciate your hard work and dedication," Mike proclaimed, pulling a small shiny box from beneath the podium. "A little something to say thank you." He handed it to Cadence.

Jackson and Phylicia stepped aside but kept their eyes glued to the gift box.

Cadence lifted a black and gold key fob and clutched it. "Is this——"

The black curtain opened, revealing the Adali SLX autonomous car.

The suits in the audience oohed and ahhed at the lustrous vehicle that wouldn't be available to consumers for another six months.

"A little something, huh," she teased.

Small feet galloping up the stairs onto the stage made everyone in the audience gasp. Cadence peered over Phylicia's shoulder at the lively little girl sprinting forward, spotting a picture of Jackson splayed on the front of her shirt. Cadence shot a scornful glance at her husband.

Hundreds of executive's hands flew to their mouths as they plucked phones from their purses and suit jacket pockets. Though Cadence didn't approve of the commotion, she didn't understand what the huge deal was with everyone taking pictures of the little girl's back. She was the only one who should've felt some kind of way since it was her husband's face plastered on the front of the shirt, not to mention the strange woman monopolizing Jackson's attention.

Mike leaned over Cadence's shoulder. "What's this?"

Her heart pounded an abstract beat. "I don't know," she whispered, never taking her gaze from the child.

Two security guards rushed in. "We're going to have to ask you to get your child and leave, ma'am."

"I have a right to be here," Braelyn exclaimed, throwing a glance at Steven as she flashed the VIP badge attached to the lanyard around her neck.

After a thorough inspection, the guard said with a remorseful tone, "My apologies, Ms. Nevels." He glanced at Mike and announced, "She has clearance."

Cadence frowned. "Nevels," she whispered, wondering why that name sounded so familiar.

"Show everyone your cute shirt, Jackie," Braelyn instructed, smiling at the pretty girl, before planting a menacing glare at Cadence and Jackson.

Jackie spread her arms wide, then faced the audience.

"Look, Mommy." She pointed jumping in place. Everybody's taking my picture." She put her hands on her hips and said, "Cheeeeese."

The lump in Cadence's throat grew larger with every word she read on the back of Jackie's shirt.

Jackson Goldsmith Is My Daddy.

Chapter 2

The plaque and key fob slipped from Cadence's fingers, bounced off her foot and clattered on the stage. The shooting pain that radiated from her big toe was minute in comparison to the agony that throbbed in her heart.

"We'll take a fifteen-minute intermission," Mike announced but put a questioning look at Cadence. "We'll have Q&A after the break."

No one moved. Cadence's orbs were transfixed on the little girl. Everyone else's was focused on Cadence.

Jackson opened his mouth to speak, but Phylicia rushed forward and snapped, "You've caused enough damage for one day." She wrapped an arm around Cadence's shoulder, guiding her toward the curtain. "Go handle your business and don't embarrass my daughter any further."

"C'mon Jackie," Braelyn said. "Our job here is done." She smiled at her daughter, then smirked at Cadence before grabbing Jackie's hand and heading toward the lobby.

"What job, Mommy?" Jackie asked, skipping at her mother's side, keeping up with the woman's purposeful strides.

Cadence halted, practically burning a hole in Braelyn's back.

Whispers of discernment rose up among people who were now more interested in Cadence's personal life than her career achievements.

"Mom." Cadence whimpered in the ladies' room. "Why's this happening to me? That little girl isn't a baby. How could Jackson claim to love me——?" She allowed the cold water to splash on her hands and wet her face. "He's been lying to me for years. What am I going to do?"

Phylicia grabbed a paper towel from the dispenser. "You're going to go back out there and finish your presentation."

"I can't face those people right now."

"You can, and you will," she commanded in a firm motherly tone. "You've worked too hard to let it all crumble at the hands of a man." She blotted the moisture from Cadence's face. "I know it hurts like hell, but this is your time in the spotlight. Don't let Jackson or that woman take it away from you."

"Mom. He had a kid on me," she cried.

"Cadence," Mike called out on the other side of the bathroom door. "I can have Steven do the Q&A if you're unable to continue. I understand."

Steven Bekker, the one who'd love to seize her position if given a chance. The one who'd *looked* the part but didn't have her level of expertise. No way would she allow him to have a nano-second of anything that was meant for her.

Phylicia squeezed her shoulders. "You can do this."

Cadence choked back the remaining tears, adjusted her suit, unlocked the door and poked her head out. Steven's robust frame was off to the side, waiting with a smirk that mirrored Braelyn's on his thin lips. "No. I'll do it."

Steven's grin fell flat.

"Alright. I'll see you in ten," Mike replied.

Her mother winked. "Show these men why you're the HNIC."

"Mom, we don't use the N-word," Cadence reprimanded.

"Okay, HBIC."

"We don't——" Cadence shook her head and glanced heavenward. "Well, I guess tonight calls for it."

Cadence rocked that Q&A even going over the allotted time to answer everyone's questions in great detail.

She'd deal with Jackson's drama later.

* * *

"I'm so very proud of you," Phylicia said as they entered the parking garage.

"Thanks for the nudge. I needed that," Cadence added, walking her mom to the car on the third level.

Cadence learned about cars while working with her dad in his body shop. They were closing for the evening when a car hopped the curb. Cadence's dad shoved her out of the way before the car pinned him against the overhead garage door, instantly killing him. The family later found out it was a drunk driver whose blood alcohol levels were four times past the legal limit. She promised to create a car that could drive itself home, so another drunk driver would never take an innocent person's life again.

"Now what?"

"Make sure that baby's his before you do anything," Phylicia cautioned.

"Why would that woman come all the way down here to cause a scene if it weren't true?"

"I know you're not that naïve," Phylicia warned. "Some women's sole purpose in life is to bring another woman down. I'm not saying that's what this is, but what other reason would she have for pulling this stunt at *your* function?" She gave Cadence the side eye. "This wasn't about her. She wanted to make *you* look bad."

"He can't come home, Momma, "Cadence said, pressing the key fob and following the answering chirps as they turned the corner. "I need some time to sort this out."

"Can we talk?" Jackson asked, from where he leaned against her car.

"What are you still doing here?"

"I didn't want to be a distraction," he replied. "I knew you needed me to drive one of the vehicles home."

"I don't need anything from you but an explanation," Cadence snapped, jabbing a finger at his face. "Mom's going to drive the car."

"I didn't do anything wrong," Jackson countered.

"Is that your daughter?" Cadence shouted, then glanced around to make sure they were alone.

"There's something I need to tell you," Phylicia interrupted, moving to stand between them. "This Braelyn woman has been to your home."

"What?" Cadence's gaze shifted to Jackson. "When?"

He raised his hands. "I've never had her there."

"She was intermingled with the guests at your anniversary celebration," Phylicia said, glaring at Jackson. "The woman's ivory skin and blonde hair stood out from everyone else. Your sister and I were trying to figure out who she was, but she disappeared before we could ask her any questions."

"How does she know where we live, Jackson?" Cadence whacked his arm with her purse.

"On everything I love," he said gazing into her eyes. "I swear I haven't seen Braelyn in six years."

"Well, I must not be one of the things you love cause that little girl goes to your school," Cadence countered, putting some distance between them. "When did you become so comfortable lying to my face? I don't even know you anymore."

"That's not my kid," he insisted.

Cadence extended her hand. "Give me your house keys."

"Absolutely not," Jackson protested, pulling away. "Where am I supposed to sleep?"

"Not my concern."

Chapter 3

The last time she was in Dr. McNabb's office the session ended with one word to balance her concerns about her upcoming marriage. *"Compromise, Cadence."*

Evidently, she hadn't *compromised* about having the children issue fast enough. She promised Jackson that she'd start a family after their fifth anniversary if he allowed her to build-up her soaring career with Adali first. Cadence's time was up. Jackson had found a way to have that family without her. Then, she had been so worried about not being worthy of him when it should've been the other way around.

* * *

Cadence showered and drank four cups of coffee before heading to Dr. McNabb's office. She didn't make an appointment fearing she wouldn't be seen right away. The Outpatient Pavilion Building opened at seven, but Dr. McNabb's office hours started at nine, so she sat in the waiting area.

An eerie feeling passed through Cadence's body as she recalled the last time she was in the patient waiting area. A beautiful woman with a messy bun holding a baby bump rushed out of Dr. McNabb's office. The expectant mother had aimed an unsettling glare in Cadence's direction. The stranger's session had cut ten minutes into hers.

Perhaps the doctor's advice and the woman's hormones weren't in sync, so that glare got a free pass from Cadence's wrath. Instead, Cadence offered a courteous smile that was met with a calculated stare.

Cadence jumped as the chiming elevator brought her back to the present.

"Good morning, Dr. McNabb."

"Hi—— good morning——" She gave Cadence a double take then checked her watch. "Did we have an appointment?"

"I'm sorry. No, but——"

"It's alright," Dr. McNabb insisted. "Come into my office."

Cadence poured what was left of her heart out to Dr. McNabb. Part of her felt guilty for being angry. Braelyn gave Jackson something that Cadence was only willing to give under specific circumstances.

Jackson shared a connection with Braelyn that he yearned for with his wife, now Jackson had it with someone else.

Is this karma?

"Excuse me," Cadence said after her phone had vibrated for the umpteenth time. "He won't leave me alone."

"Jackson?"

"Yes."

"Have you talked to him since the incident?" Dr. McNabb inquired, leaning forward.

"We don't have anything to talk about. Jackson embarrassed me in front of my employer and the entire world. He made me appear weak and not in control of my personal affairs." She stabbed an index finger in her chest. "Everything I worked for could be snatched away."

Dr. McNabb kneeled in front of Cadence and held out both hands. Cadence lowered her gaze, then slowly slid her hands atop of Dr. McNabb's.

"Close your eyes. Now I want you to take a deep breath in and hold it," Dr. McNabb instructed. "Inhale slowly. Think of what's bothering you."

Cadence chest rose, and she squeezed Dr. McNabb's hand. Tears slid down her cheeks as she felt every emotion of hurt and betrayal.

"Now Cadence, I want you to exhale slowly. Release those feelings. Don't let them rule and damage your heart. Free yourself."

As she exhaled on the last series of what Dr. McNabb coached her through, her body released some of the tension and her hands relaxed. Cadence finally opened her eyes, and Dr. McNabb was smiling up at her.

"You did great," she acknowledged, reclaiming her spot on the chair. "First, you must hear him out." Cadence prepared to protest, but Dr. McNabb held up a hand. "You may not like what he has to say but let him say it. If he's the father of this child, how do you plan on handling it?"

"I'm not sure," Cadence admitted. "I do know what it's like to grow up without a father." She paused. "But I don't know if I can welcome this child into my home."

"If you plan to stay with him, you're going to have to find a way. The child didn't ask for any of this, and she deserves the love of both parents."

"He can love on her elsewhere, just not in my home," Cadence replied crossing her legs, then realized how bitter she must sound. "Maybe one day, but today ain't that day."

"That's fair," Dr. McNabb conceded. "You have to give yourself time to heal and adjust to the new situation as well."

"The lie is what's bothering me the most," she said, scooting to the edge of her seat. "How can this man I love more than anything, lie to my face every single day? For years? If Braelyn had never shown up that night, then I would've never known. He was so comfortable living a lie," Cadence said, sighing deeply. "How can I ever trust him again?"

A knock on the door made Dr. McNabb pause in her answer. Gwen stuck her head in the room. "Your nine o'clock is here."

Cadence stood. "Thanks for seeing me on such short notice."

"I have an opening later. We can finish up then. I'll have Gwen——."

"I'm good," Cadence refused, dismissing the thought with a wave. "Thanks again."

* * *

Cadence entered Adali's Chicago Headquarters with her head held high as if last night's fiasco never occurred. She felt the stares and heard the undertones. Though it bothered her, she refused to let them know. She kept her expression pleasant and purposeful.

"Good morning, Cadence," her assistant, Jennifer

greeted. "Mike would like to see you in his office ASAP."

Her lungs fell into the pit of her stomach. She hadn't been in the building two minutes, and the shit was about to explode.

"I also forwarded all messages to your email."

"Thank you."

"Jackson's been calling all morning," her assistant whispered, following right behind her into the corner office.

Cadence turned on her heels, bumping into Jennifer. "I need you to do me a favor. Discreetly," she instructed. "Pull up anything you can find on the name Nevels. Check all positions. I don't care if it's a custodian." Cadence glanced over Jennifer's shoulder to find a folder on the shelf. "I want to know about them. And search back as far as thirty years. There's something about that name."

"I'm on it," she replied and bounced back to her station.

Cadence placed her briefcase on the glass desk, then took a calming breath before heading into Mike's office. Financially, she was in a great place, so there were no concerns. A morals clause meant they had the right to let her go. Fortunately, she wasn't the one out of compliance.

She had much to offer any automaker foreign or domestic, so she'd be able to secure another high-paying position right after suing their asses if they fired her because of the incident. Hopefully, the competition wouldn't be interested in the state of her marriage or have some deep-seated issues that would prevent a Black woman from advancing. As long as they stayed in the black and she kept making them green, everything should be cool.

"Cadence." Mike stood, gesturing toward the empty chair. "Have a seat."

She complied, crossing her legs at the ankles and waited for the words that had been made famous on The Apprentice back when at least some people liked the current resident of the White House; *you're fired.*

"There's an opportunity overseas," he said gazing out of the window overlooking the Chicago River. "Our parent company in Germany wants you there. Full time."

"Wow," she said shifting in the seat. "What an honor."

Cadence cleared her mind of all negative thoughts, realizing what a Godsend this opportunity could be.

"You've been on their radar for some time now, but your successful design and presentation sealed it for them," Mike explained. "It's an amazing opportunity."

"I'm surprised they'd still want me after that nonsense last night," she muttered.

"We've all got shit. Some stink more than others. Yours isn't any different." He chuckled, and it made Cadence smile. "They were more impressed with how you handled yourself afterward."

I need to thank mom later.

"I'd have to give it some thought. How soon?"

"Three weeks before you'd have to relocate, but they'll need your answer by the end of next week."

"Why so sudden?" she asked. Typically, we're given three to six months to make these kinds of decisions.

"They're working on a new project that needs to be completed in six months. They're confident you're the right person to execute the engineering, and I agree."

Twenty-four hours ago, the answer would've been a definite no. Jackson was climbing in his career as well. The next school term, he'd start a position in a financially stable district on the north side of town, doubling his salary and removing him from a crime-riddled school district.

Now, she only needed to decide for herself. As angry as Cadence was with him and the fact he'd cheated, she still loved him. Once again, she was presented with choosing something that advanced her career but could sabotage her marriage. But he'd already done an excellent job of that on his own.

What was she going to do now?

Chapter 4

Cadence sipped a mimosa as she prepared lunch and waited for Jackson to arrive. Three days had passed, and she felt she could speak with him without dismembering a certain male body part. Their conversation, depending on the outcome, might sway her decision to stay in Chicago with him or move to Germany on her own. She was leaning toward leaving.

They sat on the patio of their beautiful home in silence, overlooking the flourishing Japanese garden. The maple tree they planted on their fifth wedding anniversary brought Cadence back to that glorious day and everything it represented. Then she thought about Braelyn being there, tainting her home and memory.

"We had something special."

"We *have* something special," Jackson corrected her. "I haven't talked to Braelyn since she told me she was pregnant."

"When was that?"

Jackson wandered to the other side of the deck and leaned on the wooden railing. "Our wedding day."

Cadence choked on her drink.

"The child isn't mine."

"How can you be so sure?" she asked, clearing her throat.

"Because I've never slept with Braelyn."

Cadence frowned sitting the flute down on the wrought iron table. "You keep saying that."

"I never expected to see or hear from that woman again. She claimed she wanted nothing more to do with me once I married you."

"So, it was okay to fuck you while in a monogamous relationship, but not okay once you *officially* put a ring on it." Cadence grimaced, fanning the bees away from her drink. "You were still someone else's man. So where did that little girl come from?"

"I don't know ... that's the scary part," Jackson said facing Cadence. "I didn't cheat on you. Braelyn and I dated for a brief spell while we were split up, that's it. I'd broken things off with her when we got back together. She told me I'd live to regret it. I didn't know what the hell she meant. I hadn't done anything to hurt her. She wanted more than I was able to give."

"So, she has the woman scorned syndrome," Cadence said snidely. "How convenient."

"Braelyn called and told me she was having my baby. I laughed and hung up the phone. We'd *never* slept together. I thought she was trying to mess up my mind before I walked down the aisle," Jackson said, twirling his wedding band. "It wasn't until she showed up at the church eight months pregnant that I knew she'd lost her mind. Braelyn said she'd raise the baby alone. I didn't care what she did because that baby *wasn't mine*."

"And you were okay with abandoning your child?" Cadence asked in total disbelief of the man she married.

"That's not my kid," Jackson reiterated, moving closer to her. "I've never lied to you about anything, and I'm not going to start now. Baby, I promise you, the most Braelyn and I ever did was have oral sex."

Cadence brushed past him, stepped off the patio, and strolled to the maple tree. "What a joke."

* * *

"I love you," Jackson proclaimed as he wound his way past the rose bushes and the grasshoppers leaping in the foliage. "I'm all in. I have been since day one. Please don't let the actions of this delusional woman ruin our life." He stepped in front of her. "I haven't broken a vow. I'm committed to you and this marriage."

She glanced up at him, fighting to hold back the tears. Not tears of sadness, but hot angry tears at the lengths which in Jackson would go to keep his secret, even though he'd been caught.

Cadence locked a steady gaze on him. "How old is she?"

"Six."

"Damn, Jackson." She tried to move away.

"I don't want to lose you, Cadence," Jackson whispered, gripping her arm. "I love you."

"Yet, you cheated. That child had to be conceived about the time you proposed to me." She shook her head and snatched away. "Have you seen Braelyn in the past three days?"

Jackson lowered his gaze to the perfectly manicured grass.

Cadence turned to walk away, but Jackson grabbed her hand, and this time she shuddered at his touch and pulled away.

"I checked Jackie's file and had her teacher schedule a parent meeting after school."

"You're telling me you haven't seen Braelyn at Whistler dropping off or picking up Jackie? She's *never* been in your office?"

"Never. Remember, I'm the Dean of Students. I only see the kids when there's a behavioral problem in the classroom or when they're sent to my office for counseling," he added sliding his shoes across the lawn. "Jackie's not a problem child. Yes, I've seen her around the school, but I didn't know she was Braelyn's daughter."

"You mean, *your* daughter," Cadence corrected, backing away from him. "What did she have to say?"

"That it was time for me to step up and be Jackie's dad. I told her not before we take a paternity test. There's no way *possible* that I'm that little girl's father. I thought that would make her back down, but it didn't," Jackson admitted, with a sigh. "This is such a waste of time and money, but if this will prove to you that I hadn't fathered this child, then it's well worth it."

Cadence didn't know what to believe. Deep down she knew something about the situation wasn't right.

"We had the paternity test done two days ago. I paid for the test to be expedited, so the results will be in tomorrow," Jackson informed her. "We're meeting at the ice cream shop to open them."

Cadence glanced at him. "The what?"

"Cold Stone Creamery," he said. "The more public the place, the better because I don't trust her. Please come with me. I don't have anything to hide."

She hadn't told Jackson about the job offer yet. Cadence

wanted to make the decision based on what's best for her, not as a retreat from the current mess of Jackson's lies of omission and possible infidelity. They both weighed heavy on her mind and heart. The easiest solution would be to take the job in Germany and let him deal with his own plight, but something was telling her to wait. Jackson never lied before then, not even to save his own skin. Why now? Sometimes, Cadence hated her conscious.

"What makes you think I'm ready to play mommy to someone else's kid when I'm not ready to have one of my own?" she asked, gazing off into the distance, remembering the therapy session with Dr. McNabb, focusing around the word *compromise*, yet, again.

"I can imagine how this looks from your point of view," Jackson acknowledged. "But you know my heart, baby," he pleaded, searching her eyes. "I could never do anything like this to you. Please reconsider and come with me?"

"You want me to go along with this sugarcoated deception for the sake of your illegitimate child and her scandalous mother? No thank you." She stormed off. "You can see yourself out."

Chapter 5

"I'm not comfortable with this," Cadence disclosed to Jackson scanning the parking lot and lobby area as they entered Cold Stone Creamery.

As much as Cadence despised the idea of this blended family that was forced upon her and putting on a front as if everything were cool, she thought about Jackie and what she deserved.

Cadence wasn't much older than Jackie when her father had been taken away from her. Though she cherished the time they had together, it wasn't nearly enough. As a result, she was raised by a fiercely independent mother who had never remarried. But if given a chance to have her father, Cadence would love to work with him again, be a daddy's girl, and enjoy being spoiled by him. She didn't want Jackie to have the questions of *what if?* She was still young. Whatever damage had been caused could be minimalized, *if* Jackson was her father.

Five minutes later, a blue minivan pulled into the lot. The hairs on the back of Cadence's neck stood straighter than a soldier. She elbowed Jackson. "I've seen that van before."

Jackie hopped out before Braelyn opened her door. Braelyn got out, tossing her hair over her bare shoulders and rushed forward to grab Jackie's hand.

Cadence's gaze was glued to Braelyn. She walked in, and the staff greeted her by name.

"Hi, Mr. Goldsmith." Jackie ran up to him and waved. "My mom's buying me ice cream. I like Birthday Cake Remix."

"I like that one, too," he admitted with a smile. "Can I tell you a secret?"

Jackie nodded, her neon pink shirt with sequin letters glimmered under the lights.

"My favorite's Banana Caramel Crunch."

"That's my mommy's favorite, too," Jackie squealed, clasping a baby doll to her chest.

"Isn't that lovely," Cadence remarked with a smirk aimed at Braelyn who mimicked her facial expression.

"Your usual?" a woman in a black polo and khaki apron asked.

"You know it." Braelyn gave a thumbs up.

Jackie ran to the counter, her eyes focused on the place where they made the ice cream.

"This is my wife, Cadence," Jackson introduced."

"No need for formalities," Cadence interjected. "She knows who I am."

"Unfortunately, I do," Braelyn remarked in a snide tone that made Cadence want to backhand Braelyn in her smart mouth.

Jackson paid for everything, then the four of them shared a table.

"I saw you at that place where all these people took my picture," Jackie said, pointing at Cadence. "You had on red."

Cadence cringed at the memory, hoping the discomfort didn't show in her expression. "Yes, you did. My name is Cadence."

"My name is Jacqueline Nevels, but everybody calls me Jackie," she boasted shoveling a spoonful of ice cream in her mouth. "My mommy says she named me after my daddy."

Cadence gasped, glancing at Jackson then Braelyn.

"What's your daddy's name?" Cadence asked, wanting to see how far the woman had taken her plan.

"Really?" Braelyn snapped, glowering at Cadence, then turned her attention to Jackson. "You better get your wife."

Jackson sighed and threw a cautionary glance Cadence's way, which she ignored.

"I don't know," Jackie answered innocently. "My mommy said I'd meet him before I make seven."

"Do you remember when I told you, you'll meet your daddy at your new school?" Braelyn asked Jackie, sliding a white envelope across the table to Jackson.

"Mmmm hmmm." She nodded while stuffing her mouth with sweet treats. "I've been waiting for him to pick me up like the other dads, but he never comes."

Cadence's heart shattered. She felt small for acting so juvenile when this meant the world to the little girl.

Braelyn put an arm around her daughter. "That's because he works at the school."

"Uh-un, mommy." Jackie giggled. "You're trying to trick me."

"I promise I'm not." Braelyn stroked her arm. "Remember that pretty yellow shirt we decorated with Mr. Goldsmith's picture on it?"

"It was sparkly," Jackie shouted.

Yes, I remember it too. Cadence's breath caught. She closed her eyes and gripped the edge of the table until the rapid sensations jabbing needles into her heart ceased. The worst day of her life was on repeat. Jackson rested a hand on her thigh, but it did nothing to calm her nerves. It had the opposite effect.

"We put his picture on it because ... he's your father."

Cadence opened her eyes to gauge Jackson's reaction.

"How did you do this?" Jackson questioned, staring at the paper he removed from the envelope. "This isn't biologically possible."

"DNA doesn't lie," Braelyn countered with a wink.

"Let me see that," Cadence said, prying the document from his hands.

Jackie remained silent for several minutes, then asked, "Can I call you daddy instead of Mr. Goldsmith and how come you not married to my mommy?"

"I don't believe you," Cadence mumbled under her breath, pissed that Jackson had convinced her that he was telling the truth about Jackie's paternity. "How many times must you make a fool of me?"

"Can I call you daddy when you pick me up?" Jackie asked, her glacier blue eyes glowing like the moon reflecting over the ocean.

"Cadence——" Jackson called out.

"I'm not the one talking to you," Cadence sneered. "Answer your *daughter*," she remarked, shoving the test results in his chest.

"That'll be okay," Jackson replied with uncertainty in his tone.

Cadence examined the three of them closely. The paternity test confirmed what was right before her eyes. The resemblance was there, but she could see how Jackson wouldn't recognize Jackie as his child. She had an exotic look. Her skin was cinnamon like his, blue almond shaped eyes like her mom, and thick unapologetic wavy blonde hair that framed her face like a lion's mane. She was beautiful.

"Can I throw this away?" Jackie asked her mom, holding the empty bowl in the air.

Soon as Jackie danced away, Cadence asked Braelyn, "If you intended to tell Jackie who Jackson was, then why pull that stunt at the convention center? You're at the school every day. You've had plenty of opportunities."

Jackie skipped back over to the table.

Braelyn narrowed her eyes at Cadence before standing. "We're leaving."

"Already, mommy," Jackie whined. She ran over to Jackson and hugged him. "Bye, daddy."

He returned her embrace, keeping an eye on Cadence.

"C'mon, Jackie," Braelyn called out sauntering toward the exit. "Tell Dr. McNabb I said hello."

An even more disturbing reality slammed into Cadence. *This heifer's been stalking me all this time?*

Chapter 6

"What was I thinking," Cadence whispered, sitting on the park bench the following day, sipping coffee in a yellow maxi sundress with bright flowers as the early morning sun dazzled off of Lake Michigan.

She had asked Jackson for Braelyn's number. Though hesitant, he complied. Cadence could get anything she wanted from him at this stage. He was willing to do whatever it took to get back in her favor, but Cadence's focus was on Braelyn who was the real threat to her marriage. Jackson was still asserting that he *never slept* with Braelyn and she needed to speak to this woman face to face without any distractions.

"Hi," Braelyn greeted in a lackluster tone, walking up

from behind.

"Hey," she responded with more confidence than she felt.

Cadence took in everything from the woman's messy high bun, fake Versace sunglasses, pink lip gloss, down to the short denim skirt and sparkling green painted toes. She was pretty enough, although her clothes smelled like they'd been washed in stale cigarette smoke.

Something was off about Braelyn. Cadence couldn't put her finger on it. Jackson kept declaring that the timing of the girl's conception was long after they'd ended things. But DNA didn't lie. Humans did.

"Why am I here?" Braelyn asked, and had the nerve to sound irritated. "We said everything that needed to be said at Cold Stone."

"Not quite." Cadence did her best to hold her tongue. "That was about confirming your daughter's paternity—— the *right way.* This is about me understanding how you came into my husband's life in the first place."

"I don't owe you anything," Braelyn said in a snippy tone.

"You owe it to your daughter," Cadence countered. "It's not lost on me that you deliberately set out to embarrass me. You could've accosted me at any time, but you chose my job. Why?" Cadence asked, facing her dead on. "Do you need money?"

Braelyn snatched her sunglasses off. "You're one bold bitch."

"I've been called worse by those who matter." Cadence snarled, resisting the urge to punch her into non-existence. "Do you?"

Two men strolled by holding hands, walking a Yorkie who had pink bows. They were followed by a group of teenagers being obnoxious and smoking weed that was so strong Cadence almost got a contact high.

"Showing up at your job was the best way to get Jackson's attention since nothing else seemed to work," Braelyn confessed.

"Nothing else? Like what?"

"It doesn't matter," she remarked with a dismissive side eye. "We met the summer I worked at The Shedd Aquarium. I interned in the dolphin habitat for my final class and assessment before receiving my degree in marine biology," Braelyn said pulling a cigarette from her purse and lighting it. "Jackson worked security, and we became friends."

"I don't remember you from back then," Cadence remarked, flipping through her memory banks.

"You were pissed with Jackson because he didn't meet you after work and hung out with his coworkers instead," Braelyn confessed with a smug expression. "You caused a big scene and security asked you to leave."

Cadence remembered that day. Clearly, she didn't remember Braelyn. She almost caught a case because Jackson asked for a break after she was adamant about not having children. Jackson held his ground, and they were separated for some time. Cadence wanted to talk more about it, and things got out of hand, hence security being called.

"That's the first night we slept together," Braelyn revealed, and there was a flush to her ivory skin that showed she still harbored feelings for him. "We were a regular thing for months until Jackson told me he proposed to you." She took a pull from her cigarette.

Only oral, huh?

Cadence took a deep breath and held it in anticipation of Braelyn's ignorance. As expected, she blew the smoke in Cadence's direction.

"I thought we were building something," Braelyn added, crossing one leg over the other. "I was in love with him."

Why is the side chick always the one catching feelings?

"Then I found out I was pregnant," she said, Braelyn's expression could've won her an award for the best drama queen. "Jackson turned into the biggest jerk I'd ever known. He didn't even ask if I wanted to keep our baby, he just gave me the money for an abortion and told me to get rid of it."

"That doesn't sound like him," Cadence admitted

fanning the smoke out of her face and putting a little distance between them.

"I was alone and scared. I couldn't finish the last assessment because it was too dangerous since I was expecting. I didn't graduate," Braelyn said pursing her lips. "These waitressing jobs are barely making ends meet. Student loans are eating up my entire paycheck, and dammit I need some help." Braelyn paused and cut her eyes at Cadence. "Why are you staring at me like that?"

Cadence stood. "Let me tell you something——"

Braelyn bounced to her feet. "I don't want your money. I need Jackson's," she alerted Cadence, taking one last pull from her cigarette. "But if his finances are tied up with yours, then I guess I'll take yours, too." Braelyn simpered, sliding on her shades.

"You don't want to mess with me," Cadence cautioned. "My attorney will wipe the floor with your classless ass."

"I think I've proved I'm not one to be fucked with." Braelyn dropped the cigarette and squished it with her sandal. "Don't call me again unless you're handing me a check."

Chapter 7

"Jackson's on line one," Jennifer tapped on the door, then stuck her head into Cadence's office.

Cadence had blocked his calls on her cell phone, so now he was calling the office. The begging to come home and the incessant pleas to believe him saga had become too much. Her plate was overflowing with demands and expectations at work while trying to figure out Braelyn's real angle. Cadence wasn't in the mindset that a man couldn't cheat, but something about his denial—— and the reason for it gave her pause. They were at a breaking point, but even then, his claims of the timing of conception were off by three whole months.

She only had a few days left to make a final decision on taking the Germany position, and she still didn't know which way to go.

"I also have that information you'd asked for," Jennifer informed Cadence.

Cadence pressed the hands-free button. "Hit me back in five minutes." She disconnected the call, then removed the headset. "Talk to me."

"Simon and Irene Nevels worked for Adali back in the sixties," Jennifer said, handing Cadence a folder. "They had two sons, Charles and Jacob. Irene had an affair with one of the mechanics and gave birth to a set of fraternal twins, a daughter and a son. Simon refused to accept Irene's daughter because she favored her father and people would know of Irene's infidelity. He demanded Irene to give up the baby girl, but she'd left him instead and took her daughter with her. Guess that daughter's name."

Candence sunk into the office chair. "Braelyn Nevels."

"And her estranged twin is, Steven Bekker," Jennifer said, with a raised brow.

"What ..."

"Steven took his mother's maiden name after Simon died. He no longer wanted to be associated with the man who kept him from his mother and sister. The Nevels name carries a lot of weight with Adali——"

"Apparently it still does," Cadence remarked, sifting

through the papers in the folder as she recalled the night of the Global Reveal.

Jennifer continued, "He wanted to climb the ladder on his own merits, so Steven Nevels became——"

"Steven Bekker," Cadence whispered. "Damn." She cradled the papers to her chest. "Who's your source?"

"The one and only, Irene Nevels." She nodded with a smirk on her face. "Irene still loathes her ex-husband. She's wanted to tell her story for years, but Simon had threatened to cut Steven off, but now that he's deceased, it no longer matters."

A red light flickered on the office phone.

"I'll get it. More likely than not, it's Jackson." Cadence slipped the headset on and moved the hair away from her ears. "Thanks, Jennifer."

Cadence pressed the hands-free button. "Cadence Goldsmith." After a brief pause and listening to the sound of his breath, she said, "Jackson. You promised you'd give me more time."

"This is my first weekend with Jackie," he confessed, sounding a lot less like the confident man she knew. "I'm not sure how to treat this child or if I even want to spend time with her with, but I know I can't handle this alone."

She dropped the paperwork in her hand, took Jackson off hands-free, and placed the headset over her curly hair.

"Why are you telling me this?" she whispered.

"I don't know what to do with a six-year-old girl. I don't know what she likes or eats. I don't know anything."

The panic in his voice softened her stance. "Your mom's there. I'm sure she'll be able to help," Cadence suggested.

"I'm in a hotel. My parents don't know we're having troubles and they definitely don't know anything about Jackie," he admitted. "I don't know how to tell them about all of this when I'm still unsure how this woman managed to get impregnated and I'd never had intercourse with her. Baby, you know if I'd done anything remotely like this is suggesting, we wouldn't be married right now."

"You're going to have to tell your folks eventually. She's their granddaughter."

The line went quiet.

"Are you there?" Cadence asked, glancing at the display to make sure the call hadn't dropped.

"I'm here," he muttered. "I was wondering if we could stay at the house this weekend."

"Jackson ..."

Pain shot across her forehead faster than Flo-Jo crossing the finish line. Tension headaches had become that annoying friend that randomly appeared and didn't know when to leave.

"Please," he begged. "Jackie can stay in the spare bedroom, and I'll sleep on the couch."

"One moment." Cadence placed a hand over the mic.

"Yes, Jennifer."

"There's a Dr. McNabb on line two."

"Thanks." Cadence removed her hand from the mouthpiece.

She'd been anticipating that call for the past forty-eight hours. Dr. McNabb had some explaining to do. Cadence wanted to share her info and have her doctor at least be objective in walking through the scenarios.

"Jackson, I have to go——"

"I promise we won't be a hassle," he said. "I'll be out of there early Sunday."

"Sure. Whatever," Cadence snapped. "I gotta go."

She pressed her palm against her forehead, took a deep breath, then pushed the button for line two.

"Good afternoon, Dr. McNabb. I have a question for you?" Cadence said in her most professional voice. "Do you have a patient by the name of Braelyn Nevels?"

"I'm not able to disclose that information," she replied. "HIPPA laws prevent me from doing so…it's unethical."

"I know it is, that's why I'm asking," Cadence countered. "My records have been shared with this person."

"Not by me," Dr. McNabb insisted.

"So, she *is* a patient there."

"That's not what I said, and I don't appreciate you putting words in my mouth."

"She knows that I'm your patient, and a little more about

me than she should. I've never had any interaction with this woman until——"

The image of Braelyn rubbing her belly flashed in her head, followed by a pregnant woman storming out of Dr. McNabb's office with a messy bun and giving her the evil eye.

"I saw her leaving your office six years ago," Cadence whispered in disbelief. "I was in the waiting room."

"I cannot confirm or deny that because it's against the law to discuss another patient's information," Dr. McNabb defended. "You need to find another therapist. I can't have a patient who thinks I'm a liar or breached their trust."

Before Cadence could correct her error, the call ended.

How deep was this woman intertwined in their life?

Chapter 8

Cadence would give anything to wash the stench of Braelyn Nevels down the drain along with the soap scum as she rinsed her skin under a steamy flow of water. The realization that Braelyn—— and possibly Jackson—— had played her smoother than jazz on a breezy summer night was enough to make Cadence do something that would land her on The First 48.

The doorbell rang, pulling Cadence away from her murderous thoughts. She stepped out of the shower, grabbing a terry cloth robe that hung nearby. Wet ringlets of curls dripped water onto the floor creating a sloshy path.

Jackson and Jackie were on the other side of the door. They hadn't agreed on a time, but she didn't expect him this early. Cadence tugged the robe closed, tied the belt, then let them in.

Her husband's eyes danced as he gazed at her and managed to smile. "Hey, you."

"Hello." Cadence tightened the robe around her and didn't return his lustful glare. "Why are you here so early? You know I'm not usually home at this time."

"Jennifer said you were gone for the day. I tried your cell but couldn't get through."

Zeroing in on Jackie, Cadence said, "Hi, Jacqueline who everybody calls Jackie."

"Hiiiiii," she purred. "How come daddy rings the doorbell? Then she looked up at Jackson. "Did you lose your keys?"

"This is going to be an interesting weekend," Cadence mumbled after Jackie hopped over the threshold.

"Thanks for doing this." He paused in front of her, then closed his lids and inhaled. "That jasmine fragrance sure smells good on you."

Cadence held the upper part of her robe together, then turned her back to him. "I'm going to get dressed."

She slipped on a pair of running shorts, a loose-fitting crop top that draped off one shoulder, and flip-flops. Cadence wasn't going to allow Jackson to draw her into his web of charm. He always knew the right things to say and how to say them, except for this whole Braelyn situation. For that, he was saying everything that kept her confused. This weekend was about creating some semblance of normalcy for Jackie.

After chicken nuggets, French fries, teaching her how to play UNO, and watching Princess and the Frog for the second time, Jackie had finally petered out. She laid on the floor with her feet propped on her daddy's thigh, and her head resting on Cadence's lap with a draw two UNO card wedged between her fingers.

All evening, Cadence observed the way Jackson tended to Jackie. Their exchanges were natural and beautiful. If he showed this much love and affection for a daughter he just met and wasn't sure was his, regardless of what the DNA test proved, she could imagine how attentive and caring he would be to one he raised from birth. Seeing him this way had Cadence second-guessing her stance toward having a baby.

"I'll be back," Cadence said, placing a throw pillow under Jackie's head. She grabbed a fleece blanket from the linen closet and draped it over her little body.

"May I?" Jackson asked lifting a beer from the refrigerator.

"Sure," she said approaching the patio doors. "Come sit out back with me."

The crickets chirped as the warm wind blew through the garden. Jackson lit the fire pit, and they settled on the patio sectional in the midst of the serene ambiance. Cadence hated to disturb nature's groove.

"Braelyn said y'all slept together the night we broke up."

"That's not true," Jackson defended. "I have no reason to lie to you. We weren't together during that time. What would I gain in doing so?"

Cadence pondered that last question, especially knowing what Braelyn was capable of. She'd say just about anything to make Cadence feel inadequate.

"Did you know that Braelyn has been around all throughout our marriage?"

His eyebrows drew in, and she shifted so she could engage him face to face.

"I couldn't understand at the time why a woman who didn't know me could gawk at me with such hatred." She shook her head. "It all makes sense now. I didn't figure it out until today, but this was all part of her plan," she explained, finally piecing together at least part of things. "Braelyn and I crossed paths when I went to therapy right before we got married. She was pregnant."

Jackson slid his palm under Cadence's hand.

"Other than Braelyn being the mother of my child, I have zero interest in her. This whole ordeal is a mystery, and I'm scared," Jackson revealed. "I'm afraid of losing you for something I look guilty of but didn't do. I can't explain it, nor do I understand how this is biologically possible. Unless I have a twin brother, I know nothing about." He chuckled, but not in an amusing way. "Our relationship is the purest and most genuine I've ever had. I hope one day you can give our marriage another chance. I love you more than the air I breathe."

The funny thing about it was that she believed every word.

Chapter 9

The following morning, Jackie stood over Cadence shaking the bed. "Cadence. Wake up. I'm hungry."

"What?" Cadence moaned after the mini earthquake halted.

"I'm hungry."

"Where's Jack—— your daddy? Where's your daddy?"

"He's sleep."

So am I.

Cadence rolled out of bed, splashed some water on her face before ushering Jackie into the kitchen. She grabbed a box of Raisin Nut Bran cereal from the top shelf in the pantry.

"Ugh, I don't eat that," Jackie exclaimed with a frown. "That's nasty. Do you have Fruit Loops or Lucky Charms?"

"No."

Cadence traipsed into the living room. Jackson was out cold on the couch wearing a pair of plaid boxer shorts and a black wife beater. She wanted to melt all over that chocolate.

"Go brush your teeth and change your clothes," Cadence instructed. "We're going out for breakfast."

* * *

Lumes, one of Cadence's favorite spots near the Beverly area on the south side had the best breakfast around.

"My mommy used to be one of them." Jackie pointed at a woman wearing a white shirt, black skirt, nude stockings, white sneakers, and an apron. "We ate there all the time."

"Where?"

Jackie grimaced, then said, "The Pancake House, but we haven't been there in a long time."

"Why not?" Cadence asked around a mouthful of food.

"Cause she don't work there no more," Jackie answered breaking off a piece of bacon and stuffing it into her mouth. "But mommy said not to worry. So, I don't worry."

A cold shiver pricked every nerve in Cadence's body. "Where does your mommy work now?"

"Nowhere," Jackie replied stuffing in some pancakes. "We live with mommy's boyfriend. His name's Lester." Her facial expression darkened. "He yells at mommy a lot."

What if the real reason Braelyn sought out Jackson was that she needed someplace to keep her daughter safe.

"Does he yell at you?"

"Sometimes. But mommy puts me in the bathroom and tells me to lock the door. I can't come out until it gets quiet."

Cadence tried desperately not to react. She put her focus on the French toast and sausage. Evidently, Jackie needed her father in her life more than she knew. How could a little girl living under duress have such a spunky spirit?

After breakfast, they got manicures and pedicures, followed by shopping at the mall. Jackie loved trying on new clothes and was excited about her new wardrobe. Then, they visited the pet shop and bought four goldfish. Jackie said it was for each member of her family, including Cadence and Jackson. The little girl was already accepting Cadence. Despite how this little girl came into her life, she'd grown fond of the funniest six-year-old she'd ever encountered.

If this was a snippet of what motherhood was like, Cadence could picture herself doing this full-time. How could she pull it off without her career suffering?

Jackson was sitting on the front steps when they returned, wearing a sour expression.

"Look what Cadence bought me," Jackie squealed, hopping out of the car yanking the bags out of the backseat.

"Why so grim?" Cadence walked the brick path to the house.

"Where have you been?" he practically growled. "Braelyn's been calling all day to talk to Jackie, and you don't answer any of my calls. She's threatening to call the police and tell them you kidnapped her daughter."

I wish she would. "Sorry about that." Cadence pulled out her cell and unblocked his number. "You were sleep, and she was hungry. We just made a day out of it," Cadence explained. "We need to talk once we get settled."

* * *

Cadence woke up Sunday morning before daybreak, cradled in Jackson's arms, fully clothed. The Netflix home screen was displayed across the television. He moaned as she licked her dry lips that were plastered to his collarbone. The salty flavor of his skin awakened her taste buds. Her nose was pressed into the groove of his neck, twitching every time she inhaled his alluring scent. Every move created that familiar twinge between her thighs. She ached for him.

Something firm pressed against her inner thigh that wasn't there a few moments ago. She adjusted, and Jackson pulled her into him, and whispered, "I want you," as he nuzzled her ear through her hair.

Her body trembled with anticipation. There were no pertinent concerns other than the immediate need to feel her husband inside of her. She slid her hand under his shirt, then with a soft touch, strategically massaged and raked his chest with her nails. Jackson released a low guttural sound, then kissed Cadence to the point that moisture answered the call.

Jackson slipped his hands inside of her shorts, rolled them down under the fleshy part of her rear, palming her ass while grinding against her. She returned the motion tit for tat, only stopping to unzip his jeans.

"Wait," Cadence whispered, panting as she stroked his erection. "Jackie's in the other room."

He grumbled something incoherent, and she was feeling him on that.

Cadence pulled up her shorts and sighed, her erogenous zones pulsated.

"Birds and bees. She's gon' learn today." He sat upright on the couch with his erection pointing purposefully toward the ceiling. Jackson pulled Cadence on top of him, moving her shorts and panties to the side, placing the throw pillow on each side of them.

Her breath caught as she eased down on him, allowing it to fill her up. Squeezing her pelvic muscles for heightened sensation, she covered his mouth with her hand and rode that black stallion all the way to the ranch.

Chapter 10

Cadence slid into the passenger's seat and prayed she wouldn't regret the decision to tag along to take Jackie home. Jackson had posed the question after that all-consuming quickie which left her mind swooning. He could've asked for almost anything, and she would've agreed in that moment.

Three weeks had passed since she'd been touched in that way and she needed what he had to offer. After all, he was still her husband.

They drove two miles east of Jackson's school before the car slowed. The scenery changed from modest homes with manicured lawns to a string of dilapidated row houses, literally in the same neighborhood with the main street separating the demographics. Now Cadence understood how Braelyn got Jackie enrolled in Whistler. She lived in the district.

"That's my house," Jackie shouted from the backseat.

Cadence tried to tamp down the bile that crept into the back of her throat.

Torn mini blinds, broken concrete steps, scattered trash, and the shiftless inhabitants who occupied the sidewalk were enough to elicit concern.

"Is Braelyn coming out?" Cadence asked, hoping the answer was yes. No way did she want to walk past the group posted up in front of the gate. "Wow. I wasn't expecting this."

Now Cadence was presented with a dilemma. She didn't want to go into that house nor did she want to sit out in the car alone.

Jackson pulled out his cell. "I'll text her."

A minute later, Braelyn, in her blonde glory, stepped onto the stoop in floral leggings and a matching sports bra. The vagrants whistled and gawked like uncivilized heathens until a man stepped out on the porch behind her. Even the more muscular ones scattered faster than cockroaches when the light came on.

"That must be Lester," Cadence mumbled to Jackson, taking in the man's rugged, bad boy stance. He could've been fresh out the joint with raggedy cornrows and khakis hanging off of his brawny hips.

"That's him," Jackie replied, her low, shaky voice caught Cadence off guard.

Jackson popped the trunk, then left the car.

"It was nice spending time with you," Cadence said, shifting in the seat to face Jackie.

Cadence peeped Braelyn approaching the passenger side and didn't want to get barricaded in and be at a disadvantage just in case Braelyn tried something. She was out of the car before Braelyn made it to the sidewalk.

Jackie threw her body against Cadence's and wrapped her arms around her middle. "Can I come back again? We had so much fun," she squealed, squeezing her tighter.

"As long as it's alright with your mom." Cadence smiled at the affectionate little girl, watching Braelyn from the corner of her eye who frowned up from the exchange. So evidently, she was expecting daddy to step up but didn't want step mommy in the picture.

"Are you gonna save some of those hugs for me?" Braelyn asked, standing behind Jackie with a hand on her hip.

"Mommy." Jackie left Cadence and jumped into her arms. "I missed you. Cadence bought me clothes and I got my nails done like you," she rambled, wiggling her fingers. "Seeeeee."

"They're beautiful," her mother complimented, but her tone said she was far from ecstatic.

Cadence made her way to the trunk to put some distance between them. She didn't trust Braelyn, even more so because she knew from all the info that had filtered in, that Braelyn was a longtime plotter and planner. The therapist, her home, the school, her job, and who knew how many other places she'd been lurking. Plus, Cadence was leaning more toward trying to figure out how Jackson was telling the truth, not if. *How.*

Braelyn grabbed Cadence by the arm, nails biting into her skin. "Don't take my daughter anywhere without me knowing ever again."

Cadence snatched free. "Don't fuc——" She glanced down at Jackie whose eyes bore into her. "Keep your paws off of me, or you——"

"Don't you ever touch my wife," Jackson advised, shoving Jackie's bags into Braelyn's arms, pushing her away.

Lester descended two stairs. "Get your ass in here, Braelyn," he barked. She practically sprinted to the house, leaving Jackie behind.

Cadence shot a glance at Jackson and shook her head.

Jackson embraced his daughter. "I'll see you later."

Jackie planted a kiss on the crouch of his pants. "Bye, daddy."

"Don't do that," he scolded, pushing her away, then knelt and clasped her shoulders to keep her from falling. "I didn't mean to shove you. That's not a place to kiss anyone——"

"You better keep your hands off of my daughter," Braelyn shouted, causing faces to appear in the windows and some of the neighbors to come outside.

"Wait a minute," Cadence interjected. "I know you saw what she just did?"

Braelyn had the nerve to wave her off.

"What's wrong?" Jackie whined, "You don't like it?" she asked, with an innocent stare. "Lester likes it."

The bags fell from Braelyn's arms. "What did you just say?" she asked Jackie, moving Jackson out of the way. She reached out and placed a hand under Jackie's chin, lifting her face upward.

"This muthafucka's molesting my daughter?" Jackson growled, pushing past Braelyn and charging toward the porch.

"Jackson no," Cadence screamed, her heart racing faster than a galloping horse.

"Don't try it," Lester threatened, lifting his shirt to expose the pistol in the front waistband of his pants.

"Stop," Cadence yelled holding onto Jackson's waist, tripping over her feet as he pulled her small frame along.

"You must be stupid," Lester smirked. "This ain't what

you want," he said drawing the handle of the gun upward.

"Jackson. Listen to me," Cadence pleaded, gripping his arm. "You can't help Jackie if you're dead."

He froze, his chest heaved, then he glanced down at her. She tugged on his arm, and Jackson reluctantly trudged in the opposite direction.

"She's coming with us," Jackson informed Braelyn as they picked up the clothing strewn over the barely-there grass and concrete. "Get in the car, Jackie."

"You can't take my daughter," Braelyn screeched slapping his chest.

Jackie's gaze darted from one parent to the other.

He narrowed his eyes. "She can't stay here."

"You've got to the count of three," Lester warned, holding the firearm at his side.

"Either she comes home with us, or we call the police," Cadence said, ushering Jackie into the backseat, then closing the door. The little girl pressed her face to the glass. "You can't protect her."

"I didn't know," she whispered, her face was devoid of all color.

"You knew he shouldn't be around your daughter," Cadence said through gritted teeth. "As long as you're here with him." Cadence nodded in Lester's direction. "Jackie will be with us."

"You're not her mother," Braelyn scoffed.

"No, I'm not," she snapped, sliding into the passenger seat. "But she'd be safer with me than you."

Chapter 11

What have I done?

Cadence settled on the floor in her bedroom with her knees pulled to her chest. She hadn't thought things through. Removing Jackie from imminent danger was paramount. Now what? Her life didn't have room for a child on a 24/7 basis.

Jackson knocked on the door. "May I come in?"

"Where's Jackie?"

"Watching Super Why in the guest bedroom," he answered, extending a hand to help her up.

"I'm not sure where any of this is going," Cadence admitted, as they perched on the bed side by side. "My heart tells me you're telling the truth." She huffed. "I believe you haven't cheated on me, but——"

"Shouldn't that be enough. Your gut's telling you that I haven't been with anyone. You're my wife," he said clearing his throat. "And I need you now more than ever. I'll sleep on the floor if I have to. I want—— I *need* to come home. Jackie needs both of us."

"That's the other part. I know I could grow to love her. Three days in and she already has me wrapped around her little finger. But when would I have the time?" she asked with a shrug. "I have less than a week to let Mike know my final decision about Germany. This is a lot to deal with at once."

"Germany?"

Cadence sucked her teeth. "I meant to say something, but——" She paused, thinking about the gravity of her next words. "I was offered a position the day after the Global Reveal," she confessed staring into his eyes. "You weren't on my list of things to consider at the time."

Jackson stood. "You were going to just up and leave without telling me?"

"I don't know what I was going to do," she admitted shifting to pull her feet under her, again. "I still don't. I have until Wednesday."

"Wow, three whole days," Jackson said biting his lip, plopping down on the mattress. "This thing is bigger than us now. I'm going to have to accept it, but I'm uneasy because I have unanswered questions."

Silence weighed down the vibe in the room. She glanced at Jackson and witnessed a tear slither down his cheek. He was right, Jackie was part of the equation whether they were prepared or not.

"I'll schedule Jackie a doctor's appointment in the morning," Cadence said. "We need to see if she's been violated."

"I'll get some of my cousins who are 'bout that life, and we'll take his ass out." Jackson's eyebrows furrowed. "Lester's not the only one carrying heat."

"I'm praying it doesn't come to that," Cadence commented, offering Jackson a tissue, but seeing a side of him she'd never seen.

"Drama. So much easier to give a child to an anonymous woman who actually wants one, rather than one who's using her to get——"

"Wait. What do you mean *give* a child?"

"I donated sperm in college. Low on funds and all that. They love intelligent men."

Cadence pondered that a moment. "Does Braelyn know that?" she asked, her voice cracking.

"We talked about that one night," Jackson recalled, "We were swapping broke ass college student stories to see who struggled the most. Braelyn told me she used to donate blood every other month to cover bus fare. What does that …"

"Does she know where…"

"At the same hospital. That was the most logical choice since it was near campus."

"I'll be damned."

Jackson stared at Cadence, and the realization kicked in. "You don't think she …"

"What else could it be?" Cadence said gazing at her wedding ring. "If what you proclaim is true, that you've never slept with her, yet your DNA supposedly runs through Jackie's veins …" Cadence grew silent, committing her next move to her mental Rolodex.

"Jackie needs to see a therapist," Cadence said, putting her focus back on the main issue. "She did that so comfortably in front of everyone that I don't think she even realizes it's wrong." Cadence swept her fingertips across Jackson's knuckles. "I'll help with her as much as I can, while I can."

He moved closer and pulled Cadence into his arms. "Thank you."

Even in the despairing moment, Jackson felt good against her body. She'd always been a sucker for his touch. His breath moistened the flesh on her neck as she returned his embrace.

"You should call Braelyn," Cadence suggested. "She

needs to know what we're doing with Jackie."

"I want to strangle her right now. Putting herself in danger is one thing, but a child, is unacceptable," Jackson said, pulling the cell from his pocket. He held it out to Cadence.

"Braelyn's the kind of baggage you pray gets lost and never found," she said pushing the phone toward his chest. "I'm sure she'd rather hear from you than me."

Chapter 12

"Good morning, Mike," Cadence greeted over the phone while sitting in the car with her husband and Jackie outside of the pediatrician's office. "I'm taking a personal day. I'll be in early tomorrow to prep for our Skype meeting with Canada."

"Do you feel alright?" Mike asked. "In the seven years you've been here, I've never known you to call-in."

"Yes," she responded, lifting an index finger to her lips to silence Jackie who'd been tapping her shoulder. "I have some business that must be tended to, today."

"This deal with Canada should be your main focus, right now," he reminded her.

"It is," she countered. "I'll see you first thing in the

morning."

Cadence ended the call, then turned to Jackie.

"My mommy's here." She pointed as Braelyn approached the car.

They agreed to let Braelyn schedule the appointment for Jackie's physical. Fewer questions would be raised. They lied and said Jackie had a urinary tract infection and had passed blood when she urinated, ensuring the doctor would examine the outside of her vagina for any cuts or scrapes. Braelyn and Jackson would be in the room the entire time.

Cadence gestured for Jackson to take Jackie to the side.

"Braelyn, have a seat," Cadence said nodding to the passenger side. "I need some answers. We're about to step into serious shit, and I'm not putting my ass on the line for a lie."

"What's the question?" she asked closing the door.

"How was Jackie conceived?"

"I——"

"Don't lie to me," Cadence snapped. "You're willing to destroy my marriage because he chose me. He can't undo that. Lester could get all up in his feelings and kill every last one of us if we don't have our shit together."

"I … I um."

"Yes?"

"I was artificially inseminated with his sperm."

Cadence's head fell back into the headrest. "How did

you know it was his?"

"I paid extra," Braelyn admitted, gazing out of the window at Jackie. "The intake nurse helped me. All of it cost so much, paying her—— paying for the treatments. I ran out of money, and then my family disowned me." Braelyn sighed. "I thought getting pregnant would keep him from marrying you since he wanted kids and you didn't.

Yet he married me anyway.

"Let's go," Jackson said, tapping on the glass. "We're going to be late."

Cadence stayed in the car while the trio went inside. She'd be lying if she said it didn't make her hair follicles weak watching them stroll off like a happy family. She took the alone time to absorb what Braelyn told her and to weigh her options.

She dialed the office.

"Mike."

"Ah, you changed your mind," he said with a pep in his voice.

"No," she corrected. "I'm declining the job offer."

After a long pause, Mike asked, "Are you certain?"

Cadence closed her eyes and gripped the steering wheel. "Yes."

Although she hadn't signed up to be Jackie's stepmom, she was invested in her well-being. Cadence plucked her checkbook from her purse and wrote a check to Braelyn for twenty-thousand dollars.

Next, she called Dr. McNabb's office."

"Hi, Gwen, this is Cadence Goldsmith."

"Umm ..."

"I know, but if Dr. McNabb could give me a moment of her time, I can explain everything. Please."

After holding for a brief spell, Dr. McNabb came on the line.

Cadence explained everything in detail and gave a sincere apology. Dr. McNabb even agreed to be their family therapist. She'd also see Jackie for individual therapy twice a week once she confirmed with Braelyn.

Jackson and Braelyn swooped out of the automatic sliding glass doors, holding Jackie's hands as they lifted and swung her along. Cadence's heart lurched at the sight. All he had asked for was one child. And she would not be the first to give him one.

"Everything's okay," Braelyn said with a relieved sigh.

Cadence turned to Jackson for confirmation, and he nodded.

A calm passed over Cadence's body. They knew Lester had been doing something to her, but at least he hadn't physically damaged her body. Her mind was another thing.

"I thought I was getting a shot, but I told the doctor no," Jackie said clicking in her seatbelt. "No shots for me."

They drove to McDonald's Play Land, and the four of them had lunch. Jackie scoffed down her meal, then climbed into the play area with the other kids.

"I appreciate what you're trying to do, but I can take care of my daughter," Braelyn defended, squaring her shoulders as she held onto the check that Cadence slid her way. "She's coming home with me."

"That's not happening," Jackson snapped. "Lester isn't fit to be around her. He doesn't care about her well-being, flashing his gun. Did you even know he had a gun in the house?"

Cadence raised a hand, halting any further conversation. "And you're unemployed."

"So, you're judging me now," Braelyn snarled. "Struggling doesn't mean that I can't take care of my daughter."

"I never said that." Cadence gestured to the check. "That right there should be enough to start fresh, find a place of your own, and put some away for a rainy day."

Braelyn covered her mouth, and her blue orbs nearly popped out of its sockets.

"This right here," Jackson commented, placing a hand over Cadence's heart. "Is one of the reasons I love you so much." He leaned and whispered in her ear, "I'm going to put that back in your account tomorrow."

"Mommy," Jackie screamed, waving from the top of the

jungle gym before she disappeared inside a pink sliding tube.

"Find you a job and get back on your grind," Cadence advised, making Braelyn focus in their direction again. "I'm not trying to take your place, trust me, but no way in hell is she going back there."

"I don't know what to say…thank you." Braelyn folded the check and slid it into her bra.

"There are two stipulations," Cadence added. "We have to go to family therapy."

Jackson cocked his head and gazed at her. "All of us. Together?"

"Yes."

Sounds of laughter and kids screaming with joy echoed around them, causing Cadence to scan the area for Jackie. "And you have to allow the police to escort you to get your things from that house."

"I don't know about that," Braelyn said, frowning as she lowered her head. "Lester has a connect in the police department who tipped him off about an upcoming raid … so his business hasn't been good, and he's been taking it out on me," Braelyn confessed, slowly lifting her hair, showcasing the finger-shaped bruises around the side of her neck. "World War III will break out if I bring the police in there."

Cadence gasped.

"He'd never put his hands on me before, and I was afraid that if he'd hit me, he might hit Jackie. So, I did what I had to do," she said, covering the heinous marks. "My brother, Steven was able to get us VIP passes, and Lester came up with the scheme at the Convention Center. We planned to get as much money from you as we could," Braelyn admitted. "When I came away empty-handed, Lester became more violent and controlling. That's when I realized Jackie needed a father and a protector more than I needed that money. If something happens to me…"

"Nothing's going to happen to you," Jackson reassured. "Jackie will always be taken care of, and you have our support as long as you do right from here on out."

"And who cares if he gets pissed about the police," Cadence added. "That'll be your last time in there. Get what you and Jackie need right now, and you can purchase everything else later. We'll make sure no one goes without."

"Why are you so willing to help me after all the shit I've done to you?" Braelyn inquired, her eyes glassy with tears.

"Because I want that sweet little girl up there to be okay," Cadence said aiming a finger in the direction of the jungle gym. "And to do that, we have to be civilized and get all of these old feelings out of the way."

Jackson leaned over her shoulder and whispered, "Thanks for not giving up on us."

Cadence squeezed his hand. "This is bigger than us,"

she said gazing into his eyes, then stroking his cheek. "I'm sorry for not believing you. I should've known better."

Chapter 13

Cadence was in the middle of the Skype meeting with Canada and twelve of Adali's board members when Jennifer burst into the conference room. "Pardon me," she interrupted, briskly walking over to Cadence, then whispered, "Jackson's on line one. He says it's urgent."

She gauged Jennifer's worried expression. Her assistant knew better, so it had to be of the utmost importance.

"If you'll excuse me for a moment," Cadence said, following Jennifer toward the oversized doors, glancing upward at the wall clock.

Cadence had two hours to spare before their scheduled

therapy appointment. What was so urgent?

Mike pushed out his chair and quickly fell in step with Cadence. "Can't this wait," he grumbled with sweat glistening around the outskirts of his face. "We're in the weighty part of this meeting. You need to be here."

"I'm afraid it can't," she replied with regret. "This won't take long. I'll be right back."

"Jacks——"

"Something's wrong. Braelyn never showed up to get Jackie from school.

"What do you mean?"

"I was leaving out to meet with a parent and Jackie was sitting in the main office. I came back thirty minutes later, and she's still here. The secretary called Braelyn and didn't get an answer."

"Did you try calling her?"

"Yes," he replied. "I called and texted several times. No response. I had to disclose our situation to Principal Tate because she was on the phone with the police to report child abandonment."

Cadence covered her mouth.

Braelyn had found an apartment, but still insisted she needed to go back to Lester's for more of her things.

"That's CPS policy when a parent doesn't show without any notification after thirty minutes. I had no choice but to tell her."

"No worries," Cadence said looking over her shoulder in the direction of the conference room, finding that Mike was hovering outside of her office. When she made eye contact, he tapped his watch, then walked away. "I have to get back in this meeting."

"What am I supposed to do? Jackie won't stop crying and——"

"Take her home," she directed. "I'll be there as soon as I can."

Cadence went back inside. Steven was giving *her* presentation and going over *her* stats. He'd always been the one waiting on any opportunity to show her up, but she couldn't focus on that right now. She still couldn't believe he was Braelyn's twin.

Indeed, something was wrong. Cadence's initial thought was that Braelyn cashed that check, then skipped out, but she wouldn't leave her daughter behind. She sat quietly and listened for as long as she could before she excused herself for the rest of the day.

Mike hopped out of his seat, causing the conference room to fall silent. "What's going on with you?" he questioned, crossing his pudgy arms. "You've been distracted lately, and it's affecting your performance."

This was what Cadence had been afraid of, being judged harsher than her Caucasian counterparts for doing less than an ounce of what they did on the regular.

"Mike, I apologize. This is extremely important, and I *need* to leave. Otherwise, I'd be right here." Cadence glanced over at Steven who'd been watching the exchange with a smug expression. "Your sister's missing."

All the color drained from Steven's face, possibly from the information she shared, but more than likely from the shock that Cadence knew they were related.

Cadence left the office and shot Jackson a text. *I'm on my way home, but I'm going to stop by Braelyn's house first.*

He texted right back. *Don't you dare.*

* * *

She pulled in front of the house, the block was jumping with loud music and the neighborhood riffraff hanging about. Cadence left her car and climbed those cracked stairs with caution.

"He ain't home, but I'll give you whatcha need," a guy slurred from the sidewalk, holding his crotch.

"Stay the hell away from me," she shot back, reaching into her purse to position the keys as a weapon.

She rang the doorbell and knocked on the door several times. No answer. She waited a few minutes, then turned to descend the stairs. A gunshot, followed by a crash on the opposite side of the front door made Cadence bang on the steel again. She twisted the knob, and it opened. She stuck her head inside in enough time to see someone sprinting toward the rear of the house. Cadence jumped back, gathered herself, then entered after the footsteps ceased.

"Braelyn," she called out, stepping in something sticky.

Cadence glanced down at the peeled linoleum. Handfuls of blonde hair were stuck in a red liquefied substance. She willed the contents of her stomach to remain in place.

The back door was wide open. Swallowing the fear past the lump in her throat, Cadence inched into the living room and almost passed out.

Braelyn was sprawled out in a pool of blood, battered and beaten with a hole in her stomach, clutching a gun at her side.

Chapter 14

Cadence's lip quivered as she fumbled with the phone to dial 9-1-1.

"Ca—— dence," Braelyn gurgled speaking in a hoarse whisper between breaths. "Les——Lester——"

"Shhhh. Don't talk."

"Take—— care—— of—— Jackie. Tell—— her—— I'm——sorry—— and—— I—— love——" Braelyn's head slumped to the side.

"Hold on, Braelyn," Cadence cried, clutching the woman's free hand. "Open your eyes. Help's on the way."

By the time the police and ambulance had arrived, Braelyn had passed on to the other side. The cops questioned Cadence extensively before she could leave the crime scene with instructions to come to the station in the morning.

Cadence trembled as she trudged through crowds of onlookers toward her car.

"Cadence," Jackson bellowed from the parameter of yellow tape with Jackie arms wrapped around his thigh.

She ran over and fell into her husband's embrace. "She's gone," Cadence whispered. "Get Jackie back to the car."

Before he could comply, the paramedics wheeled a stretcher out with a white sheet over a body. The blood-spattered feet were exposed in a pair of sandals with polished green toenails.

"Mommy," Jackie wailed, bolting toward the ambulance.

They ran after her. Jackson scooped her up and cradled his daughter in his arms. She cried so hard that her nose bled. Cadence rambled through the contents of her purse and found some tissue.

"Are you gonna be my mommy now?" she asked between sobs.

Cadence wrapped her arms around them and gazed deeply into her eyes. "Yes, I would love to be, Jacqueline who everybody calls Jackie," she said, forcing a pleasant tone.

"Excuse me," said a man in dark denim jeans and a black bulletproof vest. "Are you Cadence Goldsmith?"

"Who's asking?" Jackson questioned, placing Jackie in Cadence's arms and standing in front of them.

"Detective O'Brien, with the Major Crimes Unit. We need to speak with you," he said glancing over Jackson's shoulder to Cadence, "at the Area South Police Station."

"Officer Douglas told me to come in the morning," she informed him, pulling the officer's business card from her purse.

"We have questions that can't wait until then," the detective said, resting a hand on his belt inches away from his service weapon. "Follow me."

"I'm coming with you," Jackson insisted.

"No. Take Jackie home. She needs to be away from all of this."

Cadence tried to put Jackie down, but she tightened the grip around her neck.

"I wanna stay with you," Jackie cried.

"I'll be back soon, okay." Cadence pried her arms apart. "Go with your daddy."

"There's no way I'm letting you go down there alone," Jackson demanded, grabbing Jackie's hand.

"You don't have a choice, baby. I'll be fine," Cadence said, stroking the little girl's shoulder. "She needs you more."

Cadence settled in the back of the Expedition and shuddered when her skin touched the leather seat. She desperately wanted Jackson by her side. What was so important that couldn't wait until the morning?

"I told Officer Douglas everything I saw," she said, plucking her cell from her purse. "Why are you taking me to the station?" Cadence pressed the QuickVoice app on her phone to record the remaining of the conversation because his demeanor screamed shady. She didn't want to become the next victim of a mysterious mishap while riding with law enforcement.

"There are plenty of unanswered questions," Detective O'Brien remarked in a dry tone.

"Like what?"

Detective O'Brien glanced at Cadence through the rearview mirror. "Like why were you there? Why would you write a twenty-thousand-dollar check to the girlfriend of a man who's a known drug supplier to the southeast side? Did the deal go bad?"

Cadence head spun faster than a spin cycle. "What—— my husband's daughter lived—— her mother——oh my gosh." Cadence's chest heaved at the insinuation. "What is it you think I've done?"

"We checked the recent activity on the Braelyn's phone, and there's a scanned image of a mobile check she tried to deposit a few hours earlier."

"That's unrelated."

"We call it motive," the detective said with a sly grin.

"Why would I subject myself to this if I'd done something wrong?" Cadence asked, blocking the view of the phone with her purse while recording, but keeping her focus on the side of his face.

The truck lunged forward, and Cadence's heart sank as Jackson and Jackie faded in the background.

Detective O'Brien smirked before putting his eyes back on the road. "We'll finish up at the station," he responded, stopping at a red light one block away from the crime scene.

Cadence placed an aimless stare toward the people standing at the bus stop. She only wanted to be a good person, and now she was wrapped up in a mess beyond her control.

A clean-shaven man in a brown suit wearing a baseball cap stepped off the curb and glanced down the street, only inches away from the rear window. Cadence didn't pay the stranger any attention until he positioned his face so close to the window that his breath fogged the glass. She flinched, glancing in Detective O'Brien's direction, then back at the unknown man. How could he not know someone was that close to his vehicle?

The man flashed a slip of dull blue paper with red blotches. Right away, Cadence recognized the check displaying her name, address, and signature. Her heart sank lower than the Titanic because now he knew where she lived.

The light had turned green, and the Expedition crept forward, then halted as a woman in a wheelchair slowly inched across the street, blocking their path.

The man grinned, removing his hat, unveiling fresh cornrows as he backed away from the vehicle.

Cadence flashed back to the scene of the crime, and one thing stood out—— the gun covered in blood at Braelyn's side.

She tilted her head, pointed an imaginary gun at Lester, pretended to shoot, then blew her smoking fingertips. Cadence aimed a quick glance toward the detective, then back to Lester, lowering her focus to his midsection, raising an eyebrow.

He slid a hand across the front of his waistband and frowned, patting his sides. His eyes grew larger than a teenager's who accidentally walked in on his parents getting it in.

Cadence winked as the car drove away.

Chapter 15

Lester's reaction solidified what Cadence thought. He'd either shot Braelyn or knew who did. She couldn't wait to share her theory with the detective, but she wasn't saying anything until they made it inside the police station, and she had a lawyer present to represent her interest. The hard glare Detective O'Brien periodically flashed through the review mirror made Cadence wish she had taken Jackson up on his offer to come along.

The Expedition pulled into the parking lot filled with blue and white squad cars, police vans, and traditional unmarked sedans and trucks. Cadence pressed her lips together and forced herself to breathe evenly as he drove past the entrance to the rear of the parking lot.

"Where are you taking me?" she asked, scanning the open space, wrapping her fingers around the door handle.

Detective O'Brien parked in the far corner where a row of paddy wagons obscured the view of the truck. He turned to face Cadence so fast that she bristled at his movement.

"Whatever you think you know about what happened today," he growled, narrowing his eyes. "You better fucking have amnesia tomorrow when you speak with Officer Douglas."

Every nerve in Cadence's body twinged, rendering her speechless. Pain traveled from her wrist to her fingertips as she pulled on the handle only to realize she was trapped.

Detective O'Brien glanced toward the creaking sound from the door handle and snickered, drawing his gun. "Do I make myself clear?" he asked, reaching over the seat and pressing his service weapon into her forehead.

She nodded, squeezing her knees together to keep the phone from falling which surely wouldn't escape his notice.

"Good." He swept the gun down the bridge of her nose, across her quivering lips, then between her breast. "If you're feeling brave in the morning just remember, I know where you live," he said, licking his lips while rubbing the gun between her mounds.

He replaced the gun in its holster, then hopped out of the

vehicle. Cadence released a breath she hadn't been aware that she'd been holding, grabbed her phone, and shoved it into her purse before he made it to her side of the truck.

Detective O'Brien gripped Cadence by the arm, yanking her from the seat in one swoop.

"Don't hurt me," she pleaded, trying to break free from his hold. "Somebody, help me——"

"Shut up," he barked between clenched teeth, pressing the palm of his hand over her mouth then pinning her body against the Expedition. "Don't make me do something you'll live to regret," he warned, scanning the area.

If he was that brazen to assault her in the parking lot of the police station, she was equally as determined to fight. The odds were in her favor. But then, Cadence thought about Jackson and Jackie. She had to do what was needed to survive.

"I thought you'd see it my way," Detective O'Brien said in a menacing tone as Cadence's movements calmed. "Now get the hell on out of here."

* * *

Cadence race-walked to the closest bus stop, nearly tripping over her feet as she kept glancing over her shoulder, checking to make sure Detective O'Brien hadn't followed. She wanted to call Jackson but was scared to pull out her phone, fearing that she was being watched.

An hour later, Cadence walked into an empty house. All she wanted to do was crawl into the safety of her husband's arms. She closed all the blinds and draperies, then sunk into the couch for a moment to collect herself.

She plucked the phone from her purse, and it rang, causing her to shudder.

"Hello."

"Where're you?" Jackson asked, in a worried tone. "I'm at the police station, and they're saying that no one saw you. That you were never here. What's going on?"

"Get away from that place," Cadence cried, dropping her head between her knees to stave off a wave of nausea. "You and Jackie need to come home. Now!"

"Why do you sound so scared? What did that detective say to you?" Jackson inquired, but Cadence didn't respond. "I'm not leaving until I talk to him."

"Just come home," she pleaded. "Don't confront him … you'll make things worse. Promise me."

"What the hell does that mean?"

"Jackson," she yelled, slapping her knee in frustration.

"Okay," he replied in an anxious tone, leaving Cadence uncertain of whether he would comply or do whatever he wanted.

Cadence ended the call, then out of habit, she scrolled through the opened apps running in the background on her phone. The Quick Voice app was the last one she'd used. Cadence refreshed the screen and played back the last recording. Detective O'Brien's voice came through unblemished up until they were outside, but it was clear enough that his threats could be heard. Every single one of them.

She emailed the recording to her personal and work emails. Then she called Mike to see if the Germany job offer was still available.

* * *

Fifteen minutes later, Jackson rushed through the door with Jackie at his side. "Are you okay? Tell me exactly what happened," he demanded, pulling Cadence into an embrace.

"Not now," she replied, glancing down at Jackie, then flicked her gaze back to him.

"Did he hurt you?"

"Not physically," she whispered, stepping back and squatting in front of Jackie. "You've had a really long day. Let's all take a nap then we'll figure out what we're going to do this evening. How does that sound?"

"Can I lay in your bed? Jackie asked, yawning.

"Absolutely." Cadence smiled and kissed her on the forehead.

The three of them laid down, but Jackson kept stealing worried glances in Cadence's direction. Once Jackie dozed off, Cadence and Jackson tipped out of the bedroom and closed the door. They settled in the living room, and Cadence explained what transpired with Lester and the altercation with Detective O'Brien.

"You *sure* he didn't touch you?" Jackson asked, kneeling in front of her, pulling Cadence's hands onto his chest.

"I was a little spooked," she whispered. "But I'm fine."

Jackson gazed into her eyes for a moment, then stroked a hand through her curls. "You didn't answer the question."

A heavy silence hung in the air.

"He toyed with me, trying to intimidate me," she admitted, leaning forward and resting her head against his. "But he didn't actually touch me."

Jackson let out a slow breath and Cadence witnessed his face soften and his shoulders relax— but only a little.

"I wonder how many cops are on Lester's payroll," Jackson mused, shaking his head with a disgusted expression.

"Who knows?" Cadence opened the Quick Voice app and played the recording for Jackson. "But we got him. This is an insurance policy, but it also puts us at risk," she added, nestling her head in the crook of Jackson's neck. "Mike said the job in Germany's still mine if I want it." Cadence paused, lifting to gauge Jackson's expression.

"What do you think?"

"I think we should do what's in the best interest of our family." He lifted from the couch and helped Cadence to her feet. "You're not going to the police station in the morning."

"But—"

"No, let them do their jobs and sort it all out. They'll find out that you didn't do it, and you don't have to make their job easier by putting your life—and ours—in danger." He stood, extended his hand to her and guided her from the couch. "Get all of our important documents and pack a bag. We'll stay in a hotel by O'Hare Airport. I'll get Jackie's birth certificate first thing in the morning, then apply for an expedited passport. As long as you have proof of travel, we can have her passport within twenty-four hours."

"What about your job?"

"It doesn't matter," Jackson said, lifting her chin and gazing into her eyes. "None of it—the job, the house, the cars … none of it matters. Where you go, I go."

Deadly Deception (Deception Series Book 2) by London St. Charles

"Watch out," Cadence screamed at the sight of an eighteen-wheeler barreling down the wrong side of the street, heading straight for them.

She clutched her stomach as Jackson swerved to the far-right lane, scraping the concrete wall. Orange sparks flew from the side of the car like fireworks on New Year's Eve. Jackson unbuckled his seatbelt and threw his body on top of Cadence.

"Hold on, baby," he shouted just as the truck crushed the driver's side like a compactor at the junkyard.

"Shit," Jackson roared, clutching Cadence as glass and metal objects flew everywhere. He gritted his teeth from the sharp pain radiating in his lower calf. For a split second, Jackson thought his right leg had been severed, but then, his ankle twitched.

"Are you okay?" he asked, raising his head only to get violently jerked forward, causing his front teeth to slam into Cadence's forehead.

"Ooooouch," she cried, holding onto his sides.

Jackson tried to shake off the throbbing pain that took

over his entire face from the impact just as the car got snatched again in a vicious game of tug of war. He held onto Cadence's headrest and peered over her head as the eighteen-wheeler detached itself from their vehicle, dragging the rear bumper down the street as a souvenir.

The full-sized vehicle had been reduced to a single-row bobsled.

"Are you hurt?" he asked, attempting to lift his body off of hers. Jackson was sure his full weight on top of Cadence wasn't good for the baby. He'd be lost if anything happened to either one of them.

"My insides are doing something funky," she groaned. "Like every nerve ending in my body is jumping, and I feel dampness between my legs."

Dear God, please let my son be okay.

"Are you folks alright," a masculine voice shouted, but Jackson couldn't see anyone from his position.

"My wife's pregnant," Jackson shouted, still trying to alleviate some of the pressure he was putting on Cadence's belly.

"Help's on the way," the man said, maneuvering to the side of the vehicle. He tried to pry what was left of the mangled door open, but it wouldn't budge. "Hey, man. What's your name?"

"Jackson," he replied, glancing down at her. "I think she's bleeding."

"I'm Floyd. I'm going to stay right here until help arrives."

"Cadence baby, you hear that," Jackson wiggled her shoulder, but she didn't respond. "Wake up, Cadence," he said, shaking her harder. "Stay with me, baby."

"My husband owns a tow truck company around the corner," a tall woman said, standing next to Floyd, breathless. "He's on his way with the hitch so we can get y'all out of there."

"You're not supposed to move them," another male voice said, but Jackson didn't see anyone near Floyd or the other woman. He must've been standing in front of the car. "You can cause more damage. Wait for the paramedics."

Cadence lifted her head, and Jackson let out a sigh of relief.

"Baby, you scared me," he smothered her face with kisses. "Try to stay awake."

"That's——" She lifted her arm, pointing straight ahead, then her eyes closed and head slumped.

"Cadence!!!!"

Excerpt of The Husband We Share by London St. Charles

Lauren Carter screamed and bolted upright in her bed, snatched from the reoccurring nightmare that had plagued her for years. She touched a finger to her right ear, expecting to feel a drop of blood, but found none. Damp tendrils of hair clung to her flushed face as she swiped a hand to move them to clear her vision.

"Help me please!"

That voice then, and now, still echoed in Lauren's mind along with the consequences of Lauren's mistake. Hours went by as Lauren was forced to listen to Shawn's shrieks of pain. Trapped on the other side of the door, Lauren was powerless to save the little girl who had come to depend on her for so much.

"You'd better stop screaming, or I'll kill you," a raspy voice had barked. A voice belonging to a complete stranger; a man who'd managed to sneak in through the back door of the Community Center, then hide inside the building and lay in wait for the right time to...

The twelve-year-old girl who cried out for Lauren's

help had barely survived a horrific experience that would dismantle someone who didn't have the support it took to heal. Shawn had managed to piece her life back together. Unfortunately, Lauren still felt the aftereffects.

Disoriented from the recurring nightmare, a chill from the master bedroom rendered Lauren numb. A red lace gown clung to her petite frame, wet from the perspiration that peppered her golden skin. She wrapped trembling arms about her midriff, but they provided no comfort. Lauren had watched Shawn's ordeal in excruciating detail through the sliver pane of glass the steel door offered.

"Help me," the girl screamed, but the man wrapped his thick fingers around her throat cutting off any further speech.

This time in her nightmare, tornado sirens had roared loud enough to shatter glass windows and pierce eardrums. A howling wind swept through the building as the steel bars finally receded, and the evil man disappeared, leaving a world of sadness and torment behind.

Lauren scanned the dark bedroom, panting as her heart hammered against her chest causing an ache that wouldn't subside anytime soon. The guilt threatened to swallow her whole. She had allowed fear of someone else to control her actions, making her less mindful of following proper procedures. Now, thirteen years later, she sat on her bed reliving an experience that had been all consuming to the point she had been forced to seek medical help.

She lowered her head, then took several deep breaths, watching her chest slowly rise and fall in efforts to create a steady breathing pattern.

Though the siren in her dream had silenced when she opened her eyes, some type of siren was still going strong on this side of Lauren's waking nightmare.

"What is that noise?" she whispered, and her voice seemed to disappear into corners of the master bedroom.

She focused on the digital clock on the nightstand, then shifted from the warmth under the comforter, her heart hammering in her chest all over again. When she stepped a few feet, the chilling grip of the dream loosened, and the cause for the blaring sound became that much clearer in her mind. At nearly three in the morning someone's car alarm was wailing louder than a Jessye Norman opera performance.

Lauren shivered as another chill raced through her body the moment her feet absorbed the coolness of the mahogany floor. Snatching a red satin robe from its home on the arm of a pewter suede wingback chair, she wrapped it around her body before rushing down the winding staircase and straight to the living room window. By the time she peered out of the vertical blinds, a few answering chirps had caused the noise to come to a complete stop.

She let out a heavy sigh, realizing that sleep wouldn't

revisit her so soon after such an adrenaline rush. Normally the pills would keep her in a restful state through the entire night—no matter what happened in this corner of the world.

So, what's different this time?

Something was off, and her subconscious finally registered a particular issue with startling clarity. Xavier. Why didn't she wake him before venturing down to check things out for herself? Why hadn't he comforted her when she woke up shrieking from a horror that no longer existed?

The empty feel of the Tudor home they owned on the south side of Chicago, in the Beverly neighborhood, enveloped her like several layers of fog descending over Lake Michigan. Her husband's Cadillac Escalade wasn't in the driveway parked next to the White Lexus truck he'd bought her as a "just because" gift when she had been named as one of Chicago's Leading Hair Stylists in Essence Magazine.

She tried to shake off the feeling of melancholy which settled in as she made her way through the dark house, thinking that maybe she somehow misinterpreted things.

"Oh my Lord," she whispered as a shocking reality set in. "Maybe that alarm was from his truck, and the damn thieves got away with it."

That had to be the only explanation for him to be missing in action. Since more DEA agents had been sent to Chicago, undercover work by local police was at a minimum. Xavier would have told Lauren of any new assignments.

Lauren climbed the stairs to the upper level, ran the length of the hallway, passing a red bamboo floor vase and causing it to shake from her efforts.

"Xavier! Xavier, wake up," Lauren yelled, bursting into the master bedroom. She flipped the light switch and froze; placing her hands on hips that her husband said would cause a blind man to regain his sight and dance a grateful jig. Evidently, that blind man had a better chance of seeing them right now than her husband would.

"Where the hell is he?"

Lauren's gaze swept the area, taking in the king-sized black canopy poster bed with two sheer drapes cascading down evenly on both sides. Then her fingers tipped the dimmer. Her eyesight quickly adjusted to the bright light illuminating a room designed in shades of ruby red and Charleston gray—colors that spoke to a blend of the couple's taste.

Only Lauren's side of the bed showed signs of recent use. Xavier's was as silky smooth, just as it had been the morning before. Even the scent of Edge Shave gel was barely discernable.

She massaged her temples, allowing several scenarios to run through her mind. Her husband, a Narc with the Chicago Police Department, had been involved with the kind of cases that put him in the same vicinity with high-level drug dealers, managing confidential informants, and the type of surveillance that had made his career a sometimes-dangerous engagement. Nothing she was aware of would cause him to disappear without a word. And he certainly hadn't seemed worried about anything earlier that evening. Her body tingled with the sweet memories.

Xavier had touched, teased, and tongued every part of her soul along with every inch of her buttercream skin in the shower just hours ago. Her body had trembled and convulsed, as he drove her to the point that was completely out of control. He had perfected the craft of making Lauren experience the ultimate orgasmic euphoria. Their lovemaking now was as good as their wedding night had been a little over nine years ago. Only better. Coupled with the fact that he was also loving, caring, and an excellent provider, made her the happiest woman on the south side of Chicago, if not the world.

A smile crept across her face remembering that afterward, they had spooned and fell asleep in each other's arms. She ran her fingers through wavy shoulder-length hair, frowning as she tried to recall a fuzzier time, thinking; I thought that's what happened?

The smile disappeared the moment she tried putting the pieces together, and something didn't fit. Needless to say, no matter how much sleep was lacking and how much she needed to be on point to do an early morning favor for a last-minute client, she was too wired to put her head back on the pillow.

Lauren Carter wasn't sure if she should be pissed off at Xavier for being left alone or concerned because he wasn't in the place he was supposed to be.

"Where the hell is my husband?"

Excerpt of Betrayal of Trust by London St. Charles

Ten thousand swords stabbed Cedrick's body all at once. His breath hitched in his throat as he struggled to compose himself. It had been over fifteen years since he'd seen anyone from his hometown of Reno, Nevada. Yet here he was in a Chicago restaurant wondering if the woman sitting at the table across from him and his wife would recognize him? His jaw clenched with dread.

"Excuse me," Sierra said, tapping the waiter's arm as he maneuvered between the tables. "Where's the ladies' room?"

The waiter pointed down the hall.

Cedrick pushed the gold-wired framed glasses up with an index finger, then stroked his goatee. A tense look crossed his face.

"Babe, what's wrong?" Sierra asked, standing and straightening her blouse.

"Nothing," he responded, continuing to stroke his full-beard.

She narrowed her gaze on him. "You always do that when you're worried about something."

"I'm fine," he dismissed.

"We'll talk about it when I get back," Sierra said, touching Cedrick's hand, slowly removing it from his face before walking away.

Nothing got past this woman. She'd always been able to read him, especially his discomfort. There's only one other person who had that gift, and she sat at the next table.

Cedrick unrolled the silverware from the napkin, wiped the moisture from his brow, and opened the menu as he sunk into the seat, attempting to make his six-foot-five frame disappear. While checking emails on his phone, Cedrick peered over the menu to observe the woman he could never forget.

Victoria Weiss was his childhood friend with a unique patch of curly white hair that made her unmistakable. She had a laugh that could fill all the cavernous gaps in the universe, especially those from his tumultuous Muslim childhood.

"Sorry for the wait, Chef Cedrick," the hostess apologized, causing him to flinch and knock his phone to the floor. "Chef Brasseur will be right out."

"Thank you," he replied, leaning over to pick it up.

"No worries." The hostess stooped graciously with her knees together, retrieved the phone, and placed it on the table.

He nodded with a fleeting smile, rubbing his thumb and

index finger across his goatee for the second time. His wife was right. He needed a different outlet for his anxiousness.

"You still do that when you're nervous, I see," the tender voice said with amusement from across the table. Her warm smile showed the beautiful imperfections God had embedded in her cinnamon cheeks. "I almost didn't recognize you sporting the Mr. Clean bald head and sculpted body. I see the years have been good to you."

Cedrick's chest expanded causing his ribs to hurt from the pressure and filled him with worry. Victoria was no one's fool. He had shaved his dreads the moment he and his mom fled Nevada and moved to Illinois. Still, maturity and a new appearance didn't mean anything to someone who knew him better than he knew himself.

"Uwezo Omari, you hear me talking to you," she said, standing at his table.

The sound of Cedrick's given name paralyzed him. He broke with the Muslim faith years ago. Now, he studied Christianity, had joined a Catholic Church, drank alcohol socially, had several tattoos, and ate pork. Cedrick even went as far as opening an upscale Smokehouse restaurant where he knew devout Muslims wouldn't dare enter, especially no one from his past. He thought he was safe.

"Boy, you better get up and give me a hug," Victoria demanded, placing hands on her hips.

Cedrick glanced over his shoulder toward the direction

of the ladies' room, then back at Victoria.

"Don't fret. Your lady friend——"

"My wife," he corrected.

"No disrespect intended," she replied, holding her hands in the air. "Uwezo Oma——"

"Don't call me that." He rose, towering over Victoria's slender frame. "I go by Cedrick now."

"Whatever." She flung her arms around his neck. "I'm so happy to see you. Everyone back home thought you were either dead or in jail the way you vanished without a trace." She released him, dabbing the area under her bottom lashes to keep sudden moisture from ruining her eyeliner.

Cedrick's brow dampened, and the wetness under his armpits trickled down his sides. Thankfully, he was wearing a dark colored shirt.

The visual of his father lying in a pool of blood with a fork lodged in his neck, clasping the Quran flashed through his mind. Cedrick shook that horrifying memory aside. He glanced down at Victoria.

"And it must stay that way," he whispered, releasing Victoria.

"I don't understa——"

"Don't tell anyone you saw me," Cedrick pleaded, gazing over his shoulder to make sure Sierra hadn't seen him with his old friend.

Other than Cedrick's mother, Priscilla, Sierra didn't know anyone from his life before he moved to Chicago, and he planned to keep it that way for her safety and his.

"This must be the lovely Sierra," Chef Brasseur said with a smile brighter than The Bean in Millennium Park.

Cedrick wiped his clammy palms along his pants before shaking Chef Brasseur's hand. "No, this is my friend, Victoria. Sierra's indisposed at the moment, but she'll be right back."

"My apologies. *Bonjour ravie de vous rencontrer mademoiselle*," Chef Brasseur greeted, kissing the back of her hand.

"Oh my." Victoria giggled.

Her laughter reminded Cedrick of the many times they'd played truth or dare. She'd always choose truth, then giggle because no one could make her do anything ridiculous. He had always thought playing with Victoria was unfair since she never picked a dare.

"It was nice seeing you, Vicki." Cedrick hoped she took the hint and retreated to her table. He wanted her to leave the restaurant, but since he wasn't in his own establishment, he didn't have any grounds to have her escorted off the premises.

Victoria swiped Cedrick's phone from the table and tapped the screen as if typing a text. He opened his mouth to speak just as her phone rang.

"There." She flipped the phone around. Victoria's number was splayed across the top of the screen. "I'll lock your number in, and you do the same with mine. Call me so we can catch up. I have so much to tell you about what's going on back home."

That's the last thing Cedrick wanted to hear.

Chef Brasseur glanced down at his wristwatch. "If you need a few minutes——"

A woman wearing a toque blanche hat and double-breasted jacket barreled out of the French kitchen doors.

"We have a situation," she whispered nervously over Chef Brasseur's shoulder.

"If you'll excuse me," Chef Brasseur said in a commanding tone.

"We can reschedule for another time," Cedrick suggested, catching a glimpse of Sierra heading their way. "I'll be in touch."

"*Merci*," Chef Brasseur said, pivoting on his heels, rushing toward the kitchen with the Sous Chef in tow.

"Don't tell anyone you saw me," Cedrick mumbled loud enough for Victoria to hear, grabbing Sierra's cardigan from the back of the chair. "I'll call you when I can."

Victoria's brows furrowed. "What's going on with you?"

"I mean it ... you never saw me."

She took a seat as Sierra walked up behind Cedrick. "Sorry I took so long," she said glancing in Victoria's direction. "The lines in the ladies' room were crazy."

After a slight pause and a questioning glare, Sierra asked, "Do I know you?"

Cedrick's heart jolted. He wanted to disappear in the kitchen with Chef Brasseur.

"I don't believe so," Victoria replied.

"Then why were you chatting with my husband while I was gone? Are you one of these food-obsessed-Instagram chef groupies?"

Cedrick eyeballed Victoria and gave a warning frown before turning his back on her and facing his wife.

"Sierra—— let's not do this," Cedrick stated, holding up the cardigan so she could slide her arms inside the sleeves. "Chef Brasseur had an emergency. We're going to meet at another time."

"Who is she?"

"A patron of this restaurant."

"I'm tired of these fangirls." Sierra pursed her shimmery-bronzed colored lips.

This was one-time Cedrick's local celebrity played in his favor.

"I'm begging you, please don't cause a scene. I'm trying to woo Chef Brasseur to come work for me. You confronting one of his customers is not a good look."

Sierra ignored her husband's warning. She leaned over Victoria's table and whispered, "I'm watching you."

"I hope you like what you see." Victoria snickered.

Sierra leaned back into a defensive stance.

All eyes and cell phones were on them.

Cedrick wrapped an arm around Sierra and ushered her out of the restaurant before she had a chance to utter another word or do something they'd both regret.

Excerpt of The Domino Effect: Lies Have Repercussions by Gisele Marie

Present Day

"I can't believe you would mess with her!" an emotionally charged Blaine screamed at the top of her lungs. "Out of all the shit I've been through with you, why would it be okay to cheat on me?" Anger dominated her body and simultaneously caused anxiety tremors. Feeling her bangle slide off her wrist, Blaine knew her inability to stay in control was slipping through her fingers.

I'd kill them both if I could right now. No regrets.

"What are you looking at? Both of you ruined my life. I hate you," Alyssa spat with a mixture of mucus and tears between each word.

Blaine began to count to ten in her head. If Alyssa were within arm's length when her count concluded, jail would be home for the night.

Before she reached five, Alyssa grabbed her purse and stumbled out of the front door. She turned to face Javier, who stood next to her with closed eyes and his arms resting on the top of his head.

Blaine could only blame herself. Falling in love with the wrong man always came with complications, even if he claimed to be a changed or different kind of person.

Shooting daggers with her eyes, Blaine stepped into Javier's personal space. With a swift move, he firmly gripped Blaine by the forearm, then escorted her to the back door of the lounge. "Let's go."

Removing his hand, Blaine swiftly walked to the passenger side of Javier's Challenger. After flopping her body into the front seat, Blaine tried to express her pain and frustration through her tears.

"Javier, I'm not understanding how you think it's okay to cheat on me. We've been through so much shit in the last couple of years. Why this? Why now?"

"I told you, Alyssa was cool," Javier assured. "The shit just happened. Sometimes, I don't think you understand why people don't care to be around you. It's always cool for you to do some shit, but other people gotta be perfect for your ass and you far from it. You didn't have a problem sleeping with me before I married Marcella and during my marriage."

For the first time, Blaine was speechless. Instead of expressing random feelings, she'd wait until they arrived home. That would ensure she had his undivided attention, and it gave her time to make a final decision about the direction of their future.

Thirty minutes later, Javier pulled into their apartment complex. He parked in their assigned spot, a few feet from the main door of the building and shut off the car. Blaine removed her seatbelt and intertwined her fingers, then turned and leaned her back against the door, giving Javier all of her attention.

Digging into his face, the pressure from his fingertips left a slight discoloration under his flesh. Nine years his senior, Blaine hoped that someday he would understand her and love her for the flaws she possessed.

Looking in her direction, Javier broke the silence first. "Babe, I have to own up to what I did. I'm sorry I cheated and hurt you. There's no excuse," he confessed, gazing directly into her eyes.

"Javier, I love you, but I can't do this. My ex-boyfriend cheated, and I promised myself I wouldn't settle for being treated how someone else sees fit. You know you—,"

Out of nowhere, the sound of a grenade exploding in a garbage can ripped through the car.

Blaine's words cut off as their car slammed into the lobby of the building; the impact whipping Blaine's head into the dashboard with force. Glass projected across the interior of the vehicle, as blood oozed from the side of Javier's head. The seatbelt prevented him from going through the windshield, but Blaine was feeling dizzy and partially incoherent.

Scanning the area for help, Javier pulled at the door handle, but his door was jammed. With fatigued muscles, he beat on the windows, searching for a way out.

Eyes glazed and ears ringing, Blaine's vision danced along the web-like lines decorating the passenger side mirror. Squinting through the hazy layer of film covering her pupils, she released a grunt trying to catch Javier's attention. Feeling her consciousness slipping, Blaine called Javier with a hoarse voice, but the active fire alarm suffocated her words.

As her neck rolled in a lethargic motion, Blaine's head rested on the door panel. Fighting to stay alert, a person dressed in all black appeared at the shattered window. Blaine struggled to focus but was incapable of recognizing any distinguishing features.

Just before she'd lost complete consciousness, the unknown individual squatted and uttered, "Damn, you're still breathing. I'll try again and do better next time."

FOLLOW GISELE MARIE ON SOCIAL MEDIA

Website: www.AuthorGiseleMarie.com

Facebook: Author Gisele Marie

Instagram: authorgiselemarie

Twitter: @authorgisele

www.ingramcontent.com/pod-product-compliance
Lightning Source LLC
Chambersburg PA
CBHW021023120726
47905CB00009B/3159